SMOKY VALLEY

Donald Hamilton

FAWCETT GOLD MEDAL • NEW YORK

A Fawcett Gold Medal Book
Published by Ballantine Books
Copyright © 1954 by Donald Hamilton

ISBN 0-449-13677-9

Manufactured in the United States of America

First Fawcett Gold Medal Edition: December 1954
First Ballantine Books Edition: September 1988

SMOKY VALLEY

1

■ After leaving his horse at Bickford's Livery, John Parrish walked up Front Street through the bright Western sunshine that still sometimes seemed to him a little too hot and brilliant for a man to endure. The sky was very blue overhead, and the dust was white and inches deep underfoot. It occurred to him that his search for health had, in ten years, brought him a long way from the red mud and the smoky skies that he remembered best from the war that had almost cost him his life. He breathed deeply now of the thin, warm air. This was a luxury that other men did not appreciate, he reflected, the simple joy of being able to breathe again without pain or effort.

A voice spoke to him. "Pleasant day, Mr. Parrish."

He stopped. Preoccupied, he had not seen Martin Coe sitting on the front step of the jail, a tall old man with a long, seamed face, a white mustache, and very pale blue eyes. His years in office had worn the silver plating from the star pinned to Martin Coe's shirt, and had polished smooth the cedar grips of the revolver strapped to his side.

"Good afternoon, Sheriff," Parrish said. "It is indeed a fine day."

"I'd get out of the street, son."

The old man's voice did not change; but Parrish had learned that out here the most you could expect, even in an emergency, was a mild warning. A man was supposed to look out for himself. Aware of a sound behind him, he took three swift steps to safety without pausing to look around. There was a high yell in the air. A buckboard, a large, old-fashioned carriage, and six horsemen thundered

7

past at a dead run, the two vehicles making a race for the stage depot up the street while the riders cheered them on.

The sheriff spat as the dust settled. "Well," he said dryly, "Anchor's in town."

"It would seem so," Parrish agreed in an equally dry tone. He brushed the dust from his clothes, trying to put out of his mind the knowledge that the buckboard had deliberately swung out to make him jump faster; he had heard the driver laugh, going by. But there was nothing to be gained by dwelling on this, and he suppressed the small, cold stirring of temper inside him, reminding himself that as an Easterner and a tenderfoot—as the people here still considered him—he was fair game for such jokes. He had not come out here to pick fights with anybody; he had had enough fighting for one lifetime.

Watching the group up the street, the sheriff spoke idly: "I hear you're losing a neighbor, Mr. Parrish."

"That's right," Parrish said. "Jack Mahoney sold his place a few days ago."

"Fine people, the Mahoneys."

Parrish nodded. "They were very kind to me while I was ill."

"Yes," the sheriff said in an absent-minded way, "fine people."

He glanced up at Parrish, and seemed to hesitate, as if weighing a matter in his mind. The younger man felt the pale-blue eyes study him carefully, noting in particular, it seemed, his lack of height and the absence of a gun. Parrish endured the scrutiny without resentment; in the three years he had been here he had become used to the way these people tended to dismiss as insignificant any man who was not weighed down with firearms, unless he was at least six and a half feet tall and suitably wide to match.

There had been a time in John Parrish's life when he had felt a need to compensate for his relatively slight build and pleasant, boyish appearance—he had been a belligerent kid, he remembered, when he joined the army. But the war had taught him many things. Having learned his own capabilities thoroughly, he no longer had any urge to demonstrate them to others; and he never disturbed himself nowadays over what impression he might be making here by not wearing a gun as the fashion of the country demanded.

The sheriff put aside whatever he had been about to say, and said instead, "Well, I will not keep you, son. Give Miss Vail my regards, if you should happen to meet her." The last words were spoken in the tolerantly amused way in which older men referred to the romantic vagaries of youth.

Parrish raised his hat and went on, vaguely puzzled as to why Martin Coe, who had never shown him any particular friendship before, had chosen to stop him on the street today; and what the sheriff had been intending to say that he had decided not to say after all. But the sheriff's motives in everything he did were obscured, for an outsider—as were the motives of everyone else in this place—by old feuds and loyalties that went back twenty years and more to the time cattle had first been brought into the Big Gun River Basin in the wake of the gold rush. Now the farmers with their plows were complicating an already tangled situation, forming an uneasy and insecure settlement of sorts near the south end of the valley; and the only thing that was clear was that the time would soon come when a young man from the East with peaceful intentions would be wise to get his money out of a ranch that had served his purpose and go back to people of his own kind, leaving these violent folk to settle their differences in their own way.

Parrish put the problem of the sheriff's behavior aside. Ahead of him, the riders who had passed him had dismounted by the stage depot. They were a hard-looking crew, typical of the kind of men the big Anchor ranch liked to hire. The leader was a thin, dark boy whose clothes and equipment made him conspicuous among the others, more casually dressed. He was wearing a black hat and a black, double-breasted shirt liberally trimmed with silver. His boots were as ornate as his shirt; and he carried about his narrow hips a heavy, carved, and silver-mounted double gunbelt supporting two large revolvers with carved ivory grips.

9

Parrish frowned at the lounging men, and at the heavily armed boy in black. A warning sense that had served him well during the war came to his aid now; he understood that if he continued along this side of the street and passed the knot of riders closely, one of them would either put out a foot to trip him or make some remark that he would have difficulty in overlooking. He drew a long, impatient breath; it was always like this, of late, and he was finding it a strain on his temper to steer a careful middle course between the kind of senseless pride that would provoke trouble and the kind of caution that, taken for cowardice, would simply encourage further persecution.

He turned abruptly and strode across the street, hearing someone behind him laugh mockingly. Not trusting himself, he did not look around until he had turned the corner at the bank and started up Hill Street. Then he paused and glanced back, half hoping against common sense that one of the Anchor riders would appear behind him, but none did. Slowly Parrish's hands relaxed at his sides. He was not a man to nurse his anger long, and good humor returned to him gradually as he continued on his way toward the upper part of town, which always pleased him with its signs of growth and progress.

Logasa was a T-shaped town, the cross-member of the T being Front Street, along the old stage road that might one day, rumor said, become a railroad. Here was the old town as it had been since the early days of the country, a rough town of saloons and gambling halls. In the daytime during the week Front Street was a relatively silent dusty thoroughfare where only the jail, the bank, and Southall's hardware store showed signs of life. At night and on Saturday Front Street awoke, within limits prescribed by Sheriff Coe, and the results could be startling to an Easterner, even one who considered that four years of war had taught him most of what there was to know about the rougher side of human nature.

But when you turned the corner at the bank, or at Southall's store, depending upon the direction from which you were coming, and walked up the incline of Hill Street —the shaft of the T—you were in the newer and more respectable part of town; the part that slept at night and went to church on Sunday. When you left Front Street behind, you were in a town that John Parrish felt he could learn to know in time; a town that resembled, not the New York where he had most recently lived, perhaps, but the small New England town in which he had been born. The sun was brighter here, the streets were wider and dustier, the people were more tanned and wore somewhat different clothes; but there was a noticeable similarity in the frugal, weathered appearance of the stores and the neatness of the small houses in which the townspeople lived, and of the two white churches in which they worshipped. This portion of Logasa was always reassuring to John Parrish, with its hint that people were pretty much the same the country over; perhaps the world over.

He walked up the hill, taking pleasure in the effort required. It had not been very long ago that any slope or stairway had been a tremendous obstacle demanding all his strength and determination. He could remember quite clearly a time when an expedition to town in the ranch buckboard—riding a horse had been out of the question then—had been a major undertaking to be planned a month in advance. Although the change had, of course, come gradually, it was still a new experience to him to be a well man again, after almost ten grim years during which it seemed as if his life had, for all practical purposes, been ended by the rebel Minié ball through the chest that, although failing to kill him outright, had left him at the mercy of the lingering disease for which the doctors seemed to have no cure. . . .

"Mr. Parrish."

It annoyed him to be caught daydreaming for the second time in a space of minutes. He looked around and saw the girl who had addressed him standing in the sunshine across the street, as if she had just come up the lane from Judge French's house. He walked over to her, raising his hat politely, somewhat puzzled.

"You are Mr. Parrish, aren't you?" the girl said when he reached her. "You have been pointed out to me."

"Yes," he said. "I'm John Parrish."

11

"I'm Judith Wilkison," she said.

"Yes, I know," he said, adding dryly, "You have been pointed out to me, too, Miss Wilkison."

The girl smiled. "I suppose so. We're not greatly loved, out at Anchor, are we?"

There was nothing to be said to this, and Parrish remained silent, taking advantage of the opportunity to study the younger of Lew Wilkison's two daughters, whom he had previously seen only at a distance. As the girl had said, Anchor was not loved, and the Wilkisons led their own life, apart from that of the Basin. It occurred to Parrish now that it might well be a lonely life. He was surprised at the thought. Resenting, as did the rest of the Basin, the arrogance of the Anchor crew, he had never before felt any impulse of sympathy toward anyone connected with the big ranch, in the shadow of which his own much smaller outfit was located.

She was a fairly tall, straight, rather thin girl; and her brown silk dress, although stylish and clearly expensive, had a look of fitting neither her figure nor her temperament very well, as if it had been bought for someone older and more dignified. She had a pleasantly shaped face, and her skin was clear, although several shades too dark with sunburn to conform to current standards of feminine beauty, which demanded a certain air of ladylike fragility. Her brown hair was fine in texture and generally rich in color, but in places faded almost to blondness by the sun, hinting that her present bareheadedness was not an infrequent occurrence.

Regarding her curiously, Parrish became aware that Judith Wilkison was likewise taking stock of him, in a frank and unembarrassed manner; and he saw himself, a little uncomfortably, as it seemed likely that she was seeing him: a man some years older than herself, of not much more than her own height, with a pallor that was only superficially covered by recent tan; a slight, reddish-haired, freckled, still-young man in a good but worn suit of Eastern cut, whose hat and boots would never deceive anyone into thinking him a cattleman. Watching her, Parrish saw in her gray eyes the same not quite flattering judgment that he had recently seen in the pale blue eyes of Sheriff Coe; and he made a note of the oddity of his being addressed twice in one afternoon by people who had shown no interest in him before, and whose only purpose in speaking to him now seemed to be to look him over in a derogatory fashion.

He said, rather pointedly, "If there's anything I can do for you, Miss Wilkison—"

She hesitated, then said, "Why, yes, you can tell me if the westbound stage has arrived. I was supposed to meet my sister and her husband, but I was talking to Mrs. French and forgot the time."

Parrish said, "You haven't missed them. Old Charlie Bell hasn't made that run on schedule in the three years I've been here; he was a good half hour behind me as I rode into town."

"Did you see any of Father's men around? They were to bring the carriage."

Parrish said, "Yes, I saw them, Miss Wilkison. They're at the stage depot now."

His tone made the girl glance at him quickly. "What's the matter, Mr. Parrish? Have you been having trouble with our men?"

"Why, not more than anyone else in the Basin, I suppose," Parrish said. "But you might tell them to watch where they drive that buckboard. I suppose it's only natural for them to play little jokes on a tenderfoot, like making him jump to avoid being run down in the street, but it gets tiresome after a while."

Judith Wilkison threw back her head and laughed. "Is that all that happened? Hell, they do that to me!"

Then she flushed slightly; it was clear that the habit of profanity was one for which she had been reprimanded more than once. She gave a quick look about her, and nodded somewhat stiffly as a passing man lifted his hat in polite greeting. Parrish saw that it was George Menefee, coming up the street from the bank, above which he had his office; the young lawyer gave him a speculative glance, obviously wondering what circumstances had brought them into conversation and—being George Menefee—how he could best use his knowledge of their meeting.

Judith Wilkison looked back to Parrish. Her mood had changed abruptly, and there was sharpness in her voice as she spoke again, and something close to scorn.

"If you have any complaints about our men, Mr. Parrish, why don't you take them up with my father? Or with the men themselves?"

Parrish said, annoyed, "It's a thought. I will keep it in mind." He looked around and listened. "The stage seems to be pulling in. You'll want to go down to meet your sister. Good day, Miss Wilkison."

He touched his hat, and turned to leave her, but was recalled by her voice. "Mr. Parrish."

"Yes?"

"You look healthy enough."

"Why, I feel fine, thank you," he said cautiously, sensing either a joke or a threat. "Why—?"

"We heard when you bought your ranch that you had come West because of sickness, and that you were planning to return home, wherever that is, as soon as your health would permit."

"That's true enough," Parrish admitted. "Although I didn't know my plans were public property."

The girl laughed. "There are no secrets in the Basin, Mr. Parrish. We know more about you than you think. Actually, the reason I stopped you is that I happen to know my father is planning to get in touch with you in the next day or two, and I thought I could save somebody a long ride over to Rafter H with the message. Dad was saying that he had heard you were quite well now, and that he thought you would be planning to go back East pretty soon, in which case you might be interested in coming around to have a little business talk with him."

Parrish frowned thoughtfully. There was a faint air of contempt about the girl facing him that he did not like; but what she thought of him, for whatever obscure reason, was not really important.

He came to a swift decision, and said, "Tell your father

14

that I'll be glad to talk to him, although I can't promise that anything will come of it."

"Tomorrow afternoon would be a good time," the girl said. "We'll keep the dogs on leash and see that the men behave politely."

The scorn was open in her voice now, and she turned from him abruptly and walked away down Hill Street without awaiting his answer. The dignity of her departure was somewhat marred by the slight awkwardness she showed in managing the skirts of her fashionable dress, as if she was accustomed to less elaborate clothing. Parrish watched her for a moment, and felt his resentment fading as he realized her youth; she could not be much over twenty, if she was that. It was stupid to be annoyed because a spoiled, arrogant child had for some reason taken a dislike to him. He swung around and strode up the street toward the familiar, relatively new, false front of Vail's Drygoods Emporium near the crest of the hill.

2

■ John Parrish was accustomed to think of himself as a businessman. His mother had died when he was a child, and he had been brought up by a father who had no interests outside business, except for some hunting and riding which the older Parrish had justified to his son, somewhat guiltily, as essential to a man's physical and mental well-being. Trained in this way, Parrish had returned to New York after the war as a matter of course—his wound having apparently healed—to take the place in the firm of Parrish and Wrenn to which his father's death entitled him. It had not occurred to him to do otherwise, although sometimes the peace-time world that had greeted him seemed strange and somewhat tasteless after four years of violence and excitement; and the duties that were given him seemed unimportant after the responsibilities that had been his as a cavalry officer.

But it had not entered his mind to make any change; and when acquaintances from the army, bored and dissatisfied, drifted off westward in search of adventure, he had considered it a show of weakness. The war had been a valuable experience, true; it had taught him that he was not lacking in certain qualities of courage and leadership, which was useful for a man to know; but he certainly had no intention of wandering over the surface of the earth in search of some imitation of a kind of life that had, after all, been marked by many hardships and a great deal of senseless brutality and waste.

Only the gradual deterioration of his health over a period of years, and the seeming inability of the doctors to cope with the disease that had attacked his lungs in the wake of the bullet wound, had driven him at last to give up, temporarily, the career his father had planned for him, and come out here to see if a complete change in climate could not accomplish what the medical profession had failed to do. He had bought the ranch through a reliable agent, borrowing heavily against his share in the business to pay for it. The journey by train and stage coach across the continent had almost finished him before he set eyes on the place, he remembered wryly.

But he still considered himself a businessman, temporarily dealing in cattle instead of merchandise; and for this reason it always troubled him that he could not really like Orville Vail, or become genuinely interested in the little man's commercial and financial problems, particularly since it was perfectly clear that Mr. Vail considered him a kindred spirit: a young man with an interest in business and a respect for the dollar equal to his own. Now as Parrish entered the store—quite dark in comparison to the street outside—Mr. Vail turned from a conversation with George Menefee to greet him.

"She's in back, Johnny," the older man said. "Go right

16

on back, but I warn you, you'd better be ready to duck, haha."

The warning and sly laughter meant nothing to Parrish for a moment, and he glanced at Menefee, whose heavy, rather pale, quite handsome face displayed an expression of masculine sympathy and understanding. The lawyer chuckled ruefully.

"I'm sorry if I've made trouble for you, John. I guess I spoke out of turn."

Parrish nodded without expression, and went on through the store, threading his way among the counters to the door that led to the rear. Here the Vails had lived, he knew, during their first hard years in the Basin, right after the war. But Orville Vail was a shrewd man who had seen the promise of the small and dusty town of Logasa; and he had done very well out of his understanding that women liked pretty things no matter how barren their environment. Now the Vail residence was a white frame house up the hill; and this portion of the building served as a warehouse for the store.

Parrish found Caroline Vail—a small figure on tiptoe—struggling to remove a bolt of cloth from a high shelf. He reached over her head to pull it down for her. She turned quickly. The light was poor back here, but he could see that her efforts had brought color to her cheeks and caused a wisp of fair hair to tumble over her forehead, giving her a prettily disheveled look. After a moment she pushed the straying lock into place and smoothed down her dress.

"Oh," she said without pleasure, "I didn't know you were here." She reached for the bolt of cloth. "Mrs. Irey is waiting."

"Let her wait."

Caroline shook her head, unsmiling. She was a girl who could express disapproval wordlessly; and she always made it quite clear to a man when he was out of favor, although sometimes the reason was not immediately apparent. She tried to take the cloth from him again.

He said, "I'll carry it."

"If you wish."

17

She turned away. He followed her into the store, laid the cloth on the counter, and withdrew a short distance while she completed the sale, conscious of the knowing, sympathetic smile with which Mrs. Irey greeted his presence. As Judith Wilkison had said, there were no secrets in the Basin.

When she had finished, Caroline did not come to him but, without looking in his direction, stepped forward to greet another customer with pretty vivacity. Parrish grimaced; there had been a time when this treatment would have wounded him deeply, but now it only made him impatient and annoyed with her for acting like a fool. He swung away, and went back to Mr. Vail, now alone by the big safe in the corner. Caroline's father laughed at him.

"Don't ask *me* to make your peace with her, Johnny."

Parrish grinned. "Just what the devil did Menefee tell her?"

"Oh, just that you seemed to be real friendly with the younger Wilkison girl, laughing and joking with her like you'd known her for years."

Parrish said, "One day somebody is going to get very tired of George Menefee. It could even happen to me."

Mr. Vail said, "Ah, you can't blame the boy for being jealous, Johnny. After all, he used to see a little of Caroline before you came; and he hasn't given up hoping, I guess. She gives him no encouragement, I can tell you that."

Parrish glanced at the small girl in blue gingham chatting away with an older woman at the far end of the store. "Well," he said, "if she asks, tell her I've gone down to Dr. Kinsman's office, and that I'll see her at dinner. That is, if I'm still wanted."

Mr. Vail laughed quickly. "Of course you're wanted, Johnny. Caroline's just temperamental, like her mother. Just leave her alone; she'll have forgotten it an hour from now. We're looking forward to having you. Mrs. Vail was saying to me only this morning that she always feels better on the days she knows Johnny Parrish is coming to town; it's so seldom one gets to talk to a civilized person out

18

here. . . . By the way, I hear that the Mahoneys are moving away. Mrs. Mahoney was in a little while ago to say good-by. She burst out crying, poor soul; I guess it's hard to leave old friends. That doesn't leave you many neighbors out there, does it, John? Just Silas Purdue's Box Seven and those small ranches back in the hills. I don't suppose you count the nesters as neighbors, and they're well south of your place, anyway."

"And Anchor," Parrish said. "Let's not forget about Anchor."

"I guess a lot of people would like to do that, haha," Mr. Vail said, and seemed a little startled by his own temerity in making such a joke. He went on quickly: "Well, I can't stand here all day gabbing; that's no way to get rich, eh, boy? We'll expect you tonight."

He clapped Parrish on the shoulder and moved away down the aisle, a small, round man with a bouncing gait. Parrish looked after him, frowning. His lack of warm feeling for Mr. Vail always left him with a sense of guilt that was intensified by the little man's friendliness, and by his memories of everything the Vails had done for him. It had been to their house he had been brought after being carried off the stage, three years ago. The driver had brought him clear to Logasa instead of putting him off at the ranch, since he had obviously needed a doctor's attention. The Vails had looked after him for weeks then; and later during the first bleak winter it had been Mrs. Vail and Caroline who, hearing from his neighbors that he had had a relapse, made the journey out to the ranch through the cold and snow and nursed him back to life a second time. He owned these people a tremendous debt; it was something he could not allow himself to forget.

The sunshine struck him, hot and bright, as he came outside again. He walked down the dusty slope of Hill Street and paused in front of Southall's store, at the corner, for a moment, noting that the stage had pulled out again, and that the Anchor carriage had departed. The buckboard was now standing in front of the hardware store near him, and as he passed the door he caught a glimpse of Judith Wilkison, in her too-elaborate brown silk

19

dress, talking seriously to Mr. Southall in the rear. Some Anchor hands had apparently remained in town; he recognized the familiar brand on several of the horses waiting in front of Pat Morgan's saloon diagonally across the street.

At the corner of the building he turned into the alley alongside, where a door admitted him to a dark stairway, which led him up to Dr. Kinsman's office, above the store. He closed the waiting-room door behind him firmly enough to let the doctor, in the inner office, know that he was here. Then, after a moment, he crossed to the window and looked out.

The window afforded a good view of Front Street from its lower end at Bickford's Livery to its upper end at Bushmill's warehouse, beyond which the road went on up the canyon to a pass through the Big Gun range that he had never crossed, although he had learned to recognize the notch of it from far out in the Basin. It occurred to him that he really knew very little of this country, for having lived in it three years. He knew the town and the road; he had some acquaintance with his own ranch; but that was all. Anchor was a name; the Big Gun Mountains were a jagged purple wall behind which the sun set each evening; the San Luis Hills to the east were a lower, less rugged barrier above which it rose again in the morning. He had come through them on the stage, but he had no memory of it, being ill at the time. He would see them once more on his way back East; and then this whole episode would become a memory, kept alive only by the fact that he had come here single and would leave married. . . .

"I get half my gossip just standing at my window," Dr. Kinsman said.

Parrish glanced at him quickly, not having heard the doctor approach. A small gray man, Dr. Kinsman had a knack of appearing silently where and when he chose; he also had an interest in the doings of his fellow men that he made no effort to disguise. Now he leaned forward to watch Judith Wilkison come out of the store below, followed by Mr. Southall carrying a keg of nails, which he placed in the rear of the buckboard, turning back into the

20

store for another load, the girl accompanying him.

Dr. Kinsman spoke. "Did you see the happy couple, John? It appears that everyone is getting married these days. I would say, from the bride's expression, that it had not been a very successful honeymoon; but then, I have always considered the honeymoon a barbaric institution. People should at least be permitted to become acquainted before being sent off on a trip together. . . . Hansen, on the other hand, looked as if marriage agreed with him. He has reason to feel satisfied, I'd say. A year ago he was nothing but another one of Lew Wilkison's hard-bitten foremen; the old man must have had a dozen of them in as many years, each one tougher than the last. I must say I was startled when I heard this one was going to marry into the family; it used to be a rule out at Anchor that any man that so much as looked at either of those girls was beaten within an inch of his life and kicked off the place."

Parrish said, "That might be difficult, with Cole Hansen. I would not want the job of beating him, either with fists or gun."

The doctor glanced at him, clearly a little disconcerted. Parrish remembered that out here it was considered unmanly to admit that you weren't quite certain of your ability to beat the stuffing out of any man in the country, no matter how much larger than yourself he might be. It seemed a curious affectation. He, John Parrish, had no illusions about how he would stack up against Cole Hansen. Lew Wilkison's new son-in-law was a big man who had brought with him to the Basin a reputation for effective violence, which he had not diminished as Anchor's foreman.

Dr. Kinsman laughed and said, "Well, I guess he does outweigh you some, at that, John. . . . Well, come on into the office and take your coat and shirt off, although I'm damned if I know why I bother to listen to your chest any longer. It's taking money under false pretenses." The older man's voice continued as they moved into the examining room: "It's a shock to think of either of those girls being old enough to marry. I well remember the first time I saw them."

21

Parrish laid his clothes aside and offered his chest to the stethoscope. "How so?" he asked.

"Why, it's not a time anyone in the Basin will likely forget. I had been in Logasa less than a year. When I was called to Anchor that morning, the big house was full of dead and dying and wounded men. Carlotta Wilkison was trying to care for them all with the aid of the two little girls and the cook; the riders who were still on their feet were posted around the place, expecting an attack on the house. . . . But you have heard the story, John."

"Never all of it," Parrish said. "It's not a subject people seem to discuss freely with strangers."

"After three years you can hardly call yourself a stranger, boy. Take a deep breath now. Now exhale. . . . Well, there had been night riding and occasional shooting for some time. I will not say how it started; you'll get varying answers, depending on whom you ask. I will not say who was in the right, either. It is my experience that after a little the right and the wrong of these things tend to get lost in the dust of the fighting. Here in Logasa, which wasn't much of a town then, we could see the showdown coming, and the betting—I will not say the sentiment, but the betting—favored Anchor to win. But the small ranchers were led by Walter Hard, the man from whom you bought Rafter H, and there were considerably more of them than there are now." The doctor looked up. "Don't judge Walter Hard by the glimpse you may have got of him when you came here, John. He was a tough, canny man before the liquor ruined him. He whipped the others into line with Silas Purdue's help. . . . All right, turn around. Take a deep breath. Exhale. You're lucky that ball went clean through you. If they'd had to go in after it they'd probably have killed you."

"What happened?" Parrish asked.

"Why, they set a trap out in the San Luis foothills, baited, I think, with a herd of stolen Anchor cattle. That's surmise; I don't know the details. As far as I know, no man who was involved ever spoke of it afterward. But Lew Wilkison took the bait, whatever it was, and piled into the ambush with thirty riders. I doubt that Walter Hard expected the result he got; six men dead, ten wounded, and Lew himself crippled so that he never walked again. That was the end of the Big Gun Basin war: Lew in his wheelchair and Walter Hard turning to the bottle, perhaps to drown out the memory of that night. It's a war that looms larger in the minds of these people, John, than the one you fought in. That one never seemed quite real, this far west." After a while the doctor went on: "I had known them all before, those who took part in it, and they were never quite the same men afterward: Silas and Walter Hard and Jack Mahoney, and the Peterson brothers, and several others who have since left the Basin. Carlotta Wilkison died a few months later, mainly from the shock and exertion of that morning. Lew Wilkison has hated the rest of the Basin ever since, as only a lonely man tied to a wheelchair can hate. . . . As I say, it's taking money under false pretenses," the doctor went on in a different tone, slapping Parrish on the back. "You're a damn sight healthier than I am. Take care of yourself and you'll live to bury all us old codgers, and a lot of younger ones, too; which is more than you thought when you came here three years back, eh?"

Parrish hesitated, and picked up his shirt. He asked, "Can I go back East safely, Dr. Kinsman, or will I be taking a risk?"

The doctor glanced at him. "Thinking of leaving us? I understood that you were doing pretty well with the ranch."

Parrish said, "Well, it depends on Caroline, of course; but I had never really considered making cattle my life work."

Dr. Kinsman frowned. "I'd be sorry to see you go, boy. And so would quite a few others; you have friends here, now. You'd have more, if—" The older man paused, embarrassed.

"If what?"

"Well, if you'd settle down and decide to stay. It's hard for people living in a place to really take to someone who makes it so damn clear he wouldn't have come except for his health, and that he plans to get out as soon as he pos-

23

sibly can." The doctor cleared his throat. "Medically, I can see no reason why you shouldn't go back if you want to, John. We know too little about your disease for me to give you advice that will influence your whole future. Certainly there's some risk in going back when you're doing so well here; on the other hand. I've noticed that an unhappy man seems to get sick a good deal more quickly than a happy one, for reasons we doctors haven't yet been able to figure out. So if you really feel that you belong back East, you'd be a fool to hang around here feeling sorry for yourself."

He checked himself to listen. Through the window came the sound of angry voices from the street below. Dr. Kinsman moved quickly across the office to look and Parrish started to follow, but paused to put on his coat.

"It's over at Morgan's," the doctor said over his shoulder. "The Anchor bunch has got somebody—"

A man's voice, thick with liquor and shrill with fear, cried, "I didn't mean— It was only said in a joking way, I tell you!"

Parrish, recognizing the voice, stepped to the window. On the sidewalk in front of Morgan's saloon, four Anchor riders had a fifth man backed against the wall. The victim was a stout, elderly individual in a cheap, dark suit, who held his hands carefully in sight in front of him to indicate that he had no intention of reaching for his gun. He looked, Parrish thought, as if he were holding an invisible melon.

"Why, that's Jack Mahoney," the doctor said. "The damn fool! If he had to get drunk, why pick Morgan's to do it in?" Parrish swung away. Dr. Kinsman caught his arm as he started for the door. "Where are you going, boy?"

Parrish said, "He used to be a neighbor of mine, Dr. Kinsman. His wife was very kind to me when I was ill."

He pulled himself free, strode through the waiting-room, and ran down the stairs, feeling a kind of helpless anger pull at the muscles of his jaw. There was nothing he disliked quite so much as stupidity, particularly drunken stupidity. For a man to involve himself and his friends in trouble because he did not have sense enough to take his bottle and his loose tongue to a safe place when he had to drink was inexcusable. . . . It did not occur to Parrish to wonder what he was going to do when he reached the street; the administration of army discipline had taught him that quick action was the first essential in breaking up a threatening fight, and that these situations had a way of making themselves clear as they went along. Nevertheless, he paused for an instant at the corner of the alley to survey the group across the street again. Jack Mahoney's voice reached him, fearfully eager.

"Sure," the fat man gasped. "That's right. I wasn't complaining, boys. Sure, Anchor gave me a fair price, more than the place was worth. I was glad to take it, honest. I wasn't complaining, I tell you! It was only said in a joking way. . . ."

Parrish started forward. He was aware that Front Street was filling up now with curious spectators, interested but ready to seek the shelter of the ground or a near-by doorway in case of shooting. He cast a quick glance toward the doorway of Southall's store, but Judith Wilkison was not in sight, and it was unlikely that she could be any help, even if she wished, which in itself was questionable. By reputation, Anchor was not a ranch where women had much influence. Parrish continued to walk swiftly toward the saloon, conscious of a definite sense of apprehension, not because of any fear of what might happen here—he had dealt with this kind of trouble before—but because any action he took in Jack Mahoney's behalf would inevitably make Anchor his enemy, and there was no telling where that would lead. It was with relief, therefore, that he noted a disturbance down the street and saw the gathering crowd split apart to make way for Martin Coe.

The sheriff came down the street deliberately, walking with the long, easy stride of the old plainsman who knew that God had given man legs to walk with as well as horses to ride. As he came up, he glanced briefly at Parrish, who had checked his stride to wait for the older man.

"Get off the street, son," the sheriff said curtly. "One damn fool is enough to have to take care of. What do you

25

think you can do over there without a gun?"

He swung away without waiting for an answer. At the same time Jack Mahoney's voice came, high and terrified: "I didn't say that. You heard me wrong, I tell you. I never said anybody forced me to sell. . . . No! I won't do it! You'll shoot me before I— It's murder, I tell you, murder. I'm an old man and I haven't used a gun for— You can't make me do it. I won't give you an excuse. . . . Ahhh!" The sound of the blow was solid and painful even at the distance.

"All right, boys," Sheriff Coe said. "That's enough."

The four of them swung to face him, leaving the fat man huddled against the weathered wall of the saloon. To John Parrish, watching from across the street, there was something disturbing in the synchronized movement; it was as if the four Anchor riders had been awaiting this interruption.

"Get out of here, Grandpa." The slim, dark youth in the center of the group spoke contemptuously. "This is Anchor business."

Martin Coe said, "Anything that happens in this county is my business, young fellow. Now get back to your cards and liquor or get out of town, one or the other. . . . Jack," he said, "you get the hell back to your wife and kids. For a man old enough to know better you pick the damnedest places to do your drinking."

Jack Mahoney did not move and the boy with the two guns did not look around. "Stay where you are, Fatty. We're not through with you yet."

Martin Coe looked up at him for a moment, and there was a noticeable change in his voice when he spoke again. "Son, you're all primed and cocked for trouble, aren't you? A man might even think you'd been sent here to do a job. Lew Wilkison has been wanting me out of the way for a long time; it seems he's forgotten I saved his ranch for him once after he'd got himself and his crew shot to pieces with his bull-headedness. Now he wants me to run this county for Anchor, and doesn't like it because I keep in mind a few other people had a hand in voting me into office." The old man took a step forward. "Well, get to it, son. Either pull those guns or take them off and throw them down here. Folks are getting tired of waiting for the fun to start."

He took another step forward, regarding the boy on the sidewalk coldly; and Parrish, watching from across the street, saw the youth's self-confidence crack at the older man's matter-of-fact approach. One moment the narrow figure had been ready, crouched, and deadly; then it was straightening up, irresolute, and in that moment the sheriff's gun came out of the holster. Belatedly, the boy on the sidewalk made a gesture toward his own weapons, to check it abruptly when he saw that he was already covered.

Martin Coe spat into the dust. There was no contempt in the gesture; it was simply a punctuation mark, signifying that the episode was over.

"I'll take the guns, boy," he said.

The dark youth started to speak, looked at the revolver aimed at him, and silently unbuckled his belt and let it fall.

"Kick them here," Martin Coe said, and when this had been done, he picked up the belt and said, "I'll keep them for you, over to the jail. You can stop by and pick them up on your way out of the Basin. I have a hunch you'll be leaving us pretty soon. In fact, I recommend it. Give my regards to Mr. Wilkison. Jack, you get the hell back to your family like I told you."

The fat man pushed himself away from the wall. He gave a quick and furtive look about him, as if estimating the number of people who had witnessed his disgrace; then he turned and walked quickly away. The crowd, that had drawn closer, let him through and he vanished into an alley. The sheriff looked at the knot of riders on the sidewalk above him, and holstered his gun.

"All right, boys," he said. "Have your fun. The town's still open."

He swung deliberately away; and in that moment when his back was fully turned, the dark boy moved. His left hand stabbed down toward the holster of the man beside him and came up again. Some instinct, or perhaps the

27

quick, startled scattering of the people in front of him, made Martin Coe pivot, reaching for the gun he had put away; he had it in his hand when the first bullet struck him, driving him to his knees. The boy on the sidewalk fired again, and a third and fourth time; life went out of the older man, and he pitched forward onto his face, still holding the weapon he had not had time to use.

3

■ Mrs. Vail was a small, graceful woman with a worn, pretty face and dissatisfied eyes. She always acted faintly surprised and annoyed when she found it necessary to leave the table during the course of a meal to attend to something in the kitchen, as if to call attention to the fact that she had been reared in an environment where servants attended to the details of hospitality. Returning now, she settled herself in her chair with a harassed little gesture.

"We were discussing Martin Coe," Mr. Vail said.

"This terrible country!" Mrs. Vail breathed. "I declare, when officers of the law are shot down in the public street in broad daylight, one hardly knows what to expect next! Does anybody know how it happened?"

"Johnny can tell you," Mr. Vail said. "He was there and saw the whole thing. It was that fancy young fellow calls himself the Pecos Kid, who works for Anchor. He seems to have got the job of foreman, now that Hansen's become a member of the family; although by the looks of him I doubt that he knows one end of a cow from another. A professional trouble-maker, I'd say."

Mrs. Vail sighed. "Well, I suppose he'll go free in the

28

end, with Anchor behind him. And Mr. Coe was such a nice man, too."

"Free?" Parrish heard a harshness in his own voice, and checked himself. "In the end?" he said, in normal tones. "He's free right now. Some deputy named Magruder came up afterward and asked a few questions and let him go."

"But how?"

"Witnesses—" Parrish licked his lips. "Witnesses testified that the sheriff goaded the poor boy past the point of endurance and then turned away just to trick him into a false move. They said Martin was reaching for his gun, and the Kid had to grab a weapon and shoot just to defend himself."

Mr. Vail said smoothly, "But if that's the case, John. ... Old Martin did tend to be a bit high-handed at times, you'll have to admit. He'd been the law around these parts so long—"

Parrish said, "No, it was a planned job. They deviled Jack Mahoney just to bring the sheriff over; they weren't interested in Jack. They were after Martin Coe. But he faced them down, all four of them; he cracked the Kid wide open and disarmed him. So the Kid waited until the old man was going the other way and shot him four times in the back with another man's gun."

The taste of the memory was sour in his mouth. *And I,* he thought, *I stood there afterward and let them talk the murderer free, because it was not my business.* Something made him glance at Caroline, whose eyes he had been avoiding, partly because they were playing a game that they had played before. She had received him coolly when he arrived, and had not spoken to him much since, but the slight pressure of her fingers when she greeted him, and the fact that she had changed her dress and done things to her hair was, he knew, an indication that she was prepared to forgive him later in the evening if he showed himself suitably contrite. After three years he should have known her moods well enough to play his part perfectly; but tonight he could not keep his mind on this game, after watching a brave man killed.

When he looked at her, he saw her blue eyes watching

him with an uneasy speculation that was no more a part of their little drama of reconciliation than his hard and questioning look. She glanced quickly away and he studied her reflectively. She was truly lovely tonight, with the kind of sparkle that made him, as always, wonder how this small, bright, temperamental person could be Orville Vail's daughter. There seemed to be nothing of Mr. Vail in her but her diminutive size. Tonight her fair hair was smooth and shining about her small head. Her dress had the demure and schoolgirlish look of all her clothes; the square neckline was cut quite low, but any hint of daring was instantly belied by the crisp, small sleeves, the pretty ruffles, and the unsophisticated material: some thin pink stuff dotted and edged with white.

Caroline stirred under his regard; for a pretty girl she had an odd dislike of being stared at. "I declare, I think you must be imagining things, Johnny," she said a trifle sharply. "Why, you're saying that Mr. Wilkison sent those men to town to—" She checked herself, and laughed. "Why, that's silly!"

"Is it?"

Mr. Vail cut in. "Caroline's right, Johnny. You're just upset from seeing a shooting; you mustn't go around saying things like that. If Anchor should get wind of it, it might get you in serious trouble."

Parrish laughed abruptly. "Mr. Vail, I saw too many men shot in the war for another to upset me very much; and I tell you, this wasn't an accident. Too many other things have happened also. As a former soldier of sorts, I keep feeling what we used to refer to as enemy pressure. That's what we called it when we couldn't see anything except an occasional scout or patrol but we knew that units were pulling into line across from us and something big was shaping up. Consider this: In the past few weeks this big bullyboy Hansen has married into the Wilkison family. That fancy lad with the two guns who apparently doesn't know as much about cattle as I do—which isn't much— has been made foreman of the biggest ranch in the Basin. There have been rumors that the farmers to the south have been having trouble with unidentified riders who tear up

30

their fences and put bullets through their windows at night—"

"Well, that's true enough," Mr. Vail said reluctantly. "I've talked to some of them in the store. But that's going to happen to those people any time they try to settle in cattle country; they've got to expect it."

"Perhaps," Parrish said. "But I know that none of my six hands have been doing it; and I doubt that Silas Purdue's three have time for any night riding, much as old Silas dislikes the sight of a plow. . . . And that's not the end of the list. A few days ago, Jack Mahoney sold out to Anchor, apparently not quite voluntarily. Today Hansen comes back from his honeymoon, the sheriff is killed, and I'm invited out to Anchor for a little business talk. It adds up, doesn't it?"

Caroline stirred and said quickly, "I didn't know that."

"What?"

"That you'd been—" She checked herself, and a little color came into her face.

Parrish said calmly, "Why, yes. Miss Judith Wilkison stopped me on the street this afternoon and told me that her father wanted to see me." After a moment he added, "I stopped by the store to tell you about it, but you were quite busy, remember?" He had learned that with Caroline Vail it was best always to pursue any advantage fully, and he went on: "I'm surprised George Menefee didn't mention it; he passed us while we were talking."

Caroline's glance dropped and there was a brief silence. Mrs. Vail, sensing something amiss, spoke quickly: "What did you tell the girl, John?"

"I said I would ride out tomorrow and hear what Mr. Wilkison had to say. But now—"

"Why, it's what you've been waiting for, boy!" Mr. Vail said eagerly. "Isn't it? You've been talking about selling as soon as Dr. Kinsman thought you were well enough to leave, and certainly Mr. Wilkison can afford to pay a better price for the property than anyone else around here."

"That's true," Parrish said. He hesitated, and went on: "But I'm not quite sure I want to deal with anybody who'd send four killers to shoot one old man in the back." The

31

harshness was back in his voice again. He said, "At least, if he wants my ranch, he can come to me for it, cripple or not. I'm getting just a little tired of stepping lively any time the Anchor brand shows up on the horizon."

"That's childish, boy!" Mr. Vail protested. "Just because Martin Coe got himself killed is no reason you have to pass up an opportunity to make a neat profit."

"Think of Caroline," Mrs. Vail said. "You would not want some silly small-boy pride to stand in the way of her happiness, would you, John? And I declare, I can't see how your pride is involved, anyway."

This, he thought ruefully, was why, coming to the Vails' for dinner these days, he always opened the white gate with a certain reluctance: the Vails were so eager to get their daughter safely married to him that it was a little embarrassing for Caroline as well as for him; and they also seemed convinced that her happiness lay in the East. They had been at him for months to take the final step of offering the ranch for sale. He could not help resenting their interference. It was not fair to Caroline, and it certainly showed little faith in him; and it had helped to rob their relationship of the dignity and sweetness it had once had.

Generally Parrish managed to keep his feelings concealed, but tonight he could not. There was an anger that came to a man when he stood by weaponless and ineffectual and watched another man killed in a cowardly fashion and the killer turned loose unpunished. *But after all, that's why you don't wear a gun,* he reminded himself, *so that you won't get involved in any local squabbles. This isn't your country, nor are these your people; and you haven't the slightest intention of making their quarrels your own.* But when he put it like that, it seemed a little like resigning from the human race. He heard himself speaking to Mr. Vail in a curt and preoccupied tone that did nothing to clear the strained atmosphere; and the dinner ended on a note of polite discord. Afterward he refused a drink and, as soon as he decently could, made his excuses on the grounds of the long ride home.

Mrs. Vail was startled. "But John, I thought you'd stay

overnight, hear? You always do, and I have your room all ready for you. I declare, you mustn't think of riding all that way in the dark; you'll make yourself sick again!"

Parrish said, "I'm sorry, but I really want to get back. Something's brewing over at Anchor, and I want to make sure my men stay out of trouble. My foreman's all right, but I've got a couple of hotheads in the crew who'd like nothing better than taking a shot at a Wilkison rider, given half an excuse."

Mr. Vail said, "Well, in that case I suppose you'd better go, boy. You certainly don't want to have any trouble with Anchor, no matter how you feel about Martin Coe. But frankly, if you want my opinion, I think you're making a mistake—"

Parrish said, "It's possible. I'll think it over between tonight and tomorrow. Perhaps you're right. Good night."

4

It was pleasant to come out of the house, still warm from the heat of the day, into the cool darkness; and Parrish stepped down from the porch and walked slowly down the path between the parched flowerbeds—Mrs. Vail always planted flowers hopefully each spring—to the gate. He paused there for a moment, breathing deeply of the clean air. Out here there were no cooking odors or lamp fumes or taut emotions. A glow over the houses to the east promised moonlight for his ride home.

He did not know that he was waiting, but of course he was; and presently he heard the opening and closing of the front door behind him, and the whisper of her dress as she came along the path to him. It was a victory of sorts. He had not planned it and he was not very proud of it. He turned to look at her. Her face was a small, pale, reproachful blur in the darkness.

"Honey, you hurt Mother's feelings, leaving like that," she said. It was only a trial shot, he knew, to establish whether or not he could be intimidated. After a moment, seeing that he did not intend to yield, she laughed softly. "They are kind of silly, aren't they? I declare, the way they keep at us, I get kind of provoked with them myself."

It was time for him to make a concession, and he said, "I guess I've just got out of the habit of taking advice, Caroline. I've been running my own affairs since I joined the army at seventeen."

"The Yankee Army!" she said lightly. "The way you talk about it, anybody'd think it was the one big thing in your life."

"Why, maybe it was," he said, "until I met you."

She laughed. "Honey, that's sweet of you. I like you to say things like that even when you don't mean them." Abruptly her laughter died and she shivered slightly. "Let's take a walk, Johnny. I don't want to go back in the house right now. You don't really have to get back to your old ranch this minute, do you?" He shook his head and opened the gate for her; and she took his arm, holding it tightly and walking close to him. "Honey," she said presently, "I'm sorry about this afternoon. I don't know what makes me act like such a little beast sometimes." He felt the quick pressure of her fingers on his arm. "Is she pretty, John?"

"Who?"

"Why, Judith Wilkison, of course."

Parrish shrugged. "You've seen her."

"Oh, men are so close-mouthed! I want to know what you think."

"She's just a child. Maybe she'll grow up to be a handsome woman."

"Silly, she's as old as I am," Caroline said. After a moment she went on: "Honestly, I feel real sorry for her. Think of being a big clumsy girl like that and living in the same house with someone as lovely as Martha. You'd think, though, that she'd learn *something* from watching her older sister; the way she dresses is a disgrace, considering the money she has to spend. And it's positively embarrassing to watch her in those ridiculous expensive frocks she comes to town in, striding around as if she had boots on. I declare, rich as they are, they could at least hire somebody to take the girl in hand and teach her how to walk properly."

Parrish said carefully, "Well, she certainly doesn't know how to dress; even a man can tell that."

Caroline glanced at him, and seemed to sense from his voice that he had had enough of Judith Wilkison now. She paused and glanced around. Their slow pace had brought them down the street past the last houses and out into the open.

Above the dark mass of the foothills, the towering peaks of the Big Gun range to the west were faintly silvered with the oncoming moonlight. Parrish felt a touch on his sleeve and turned to look at the girl beside him; he was startled when she came abruptly into his arms. She buried her face in his coat and he held her, waiting for her to look up. When she did so, he kissed her, and was rewarded with the quick and eager, almost wanton, promise of her lips and body that always shocked him a little even as it intrigued him, since it was in such marked contrast to the prim and dainty prettiness of her outward appearance. After the kiss, he held her close, felt her tremble, and realized that she was crying.

"What's the matter?" he asked. "What's the matter, Caroline?"

She shook her head mutely. After a little she freed herself, found a small handkerchief in her bodice, and dried her eyes.

"I'm s-sorry, honey," she breathed. "I declare, I don't know what's g-got into me tonight." She tucked the handkerchief away, touched back a straying tendril of hair, and managed a smile. "Let's not go back just yet. Let's walk out there a ways. I get so sick of this town and everybody in it. I could scream!"

35

He glanced at the dim slope of the ridge above them. Although there had been no Indian troubles in the Basin since the war, he had never considered it advisable to wander about this country afoot, particularly after dark; but it seemed unromantic and a little cowardly to say so. He said, "Your dress—"

"Ah, it's just an old one; I don't care what happens to it." Doubting the truth of this statement, Parrish glanced at her quickly. She said, with sudden sharpness, "Of course, if you're tired of my company, John Parrish, you're free to take me home. I wouldn't dream of imposing on your patience!"

He laughed and took her arm; and after a moment the anger went out of her, she giggled at her own temper, and leaned against him briefly in the way she had of indicating that all was well between them again. A few yards from the end of the lane they had to pause for her to gather up her ruffled skirts that kept catching in the low growth. They continued up the slope, topped the nearest rise, and paused for breath. Caroline glanced about her and moved toward a spot where two of the desert junipers, growing more closely together than was usual with these sprawling, stunted little trees, made a sheltered place. Parrish followed, watching as she seated herself and made the usual feminine gesture toward her hair.

"I declare—" Her voice came to him, softly laughing. "I declare, it's a good thing it's dark; I must look a fright."

He had never been alone with her like this before in all the three years he had known her. It was too dark for him to make out the little white dots in the starched pink material of her dress, or even the color of the cloth; but he could distinguish the whiteness of her bare arms and throat, and he could determine the shape of her small face although he could not read its expression.

"Johnny," she whispered, "honey, you'll do it for me, won't you?"

"Do what?"

"Ride to Anchor tomorrow and talk to Mr. Wilkison. Please!" She caught him by the shoulders, leaning close to him. "You don't know what it means to me," she breathed.

36

"I hate this country, honey; I just hate it so! If you—if you'll take me out of it, I'll be grateful all the rest of my life. I'll see that you never regret it for a minute!"

She was not usually a humble girl, and the unwonted humility of this declaration disturbed him. He could think of nothing suitable to say and, instead of speaking, he drew her to him. Her arms went about his neck, and her lips were urgent and possessive against his; the last vestige of restraint seemed to leave her then, and her small body yielded beneath his hands, lying against him hard as he kissed her. At last she flung back her head to look at him, her mouth strained in the dusk, her eyes wide and dark in her dim face. They were both breathing unnaturally.

"Honey," she gasped. "We shouldn't, we mustn't—"

The hypocrisy of this, coming from her, who had brought him here, angered him unreasonably; and the anger was his final undoing. It combined with all the irritations and annoyances of the long day in a sudden wave of feeling that swept away, in an instant, all the carefully tended barriers of his restraint. A familiar impulse which tonight he could not check made him pull his hand roughly across her shoulder, baring her shoulder and breast to his caress; even then, part of his mind remained aloof from the act, prepared to retreat and humbly apologize at the first sign of displeasure from her; but Caroline responded to the touch of his hands and the pressure of his lips, and let herself be pushed back onto the dusty ground with only a brief gasp of protest, and this not at the indignity but merely at the audible damage to her clothing. Then this, too, was forgotten, and her small hands, strong and urgent, were drawing him down to her hard, and he was searching for and finding her among the crisp, starched skirts and petticoats, heedlessly crushed and disordered now; and they were alone for a period of time in a breathless, rushing darkness that had no stars. . . .

When they returned to the end of the street, the moon was up. They stopped to give Caroline another opportunity to make repairs; and she did so, laughing a little at her own dusty dishevelment.

"Honey, I'm a sight!" she whispered. "I hope you're

ashamed of yourself, hear?" She straightened up, presented herself for kissing, and clung to him for a moment. "You'll go to Anchor in the morning, honey?"

"My invitation was for the afternoon," he said dryly. "Yes, I'll ride to Anchor tomorrow, Caroline."

"And you *will* sell, if he wants to buy."

"I'll accept any fair price he offers me," Parrish promised. They walked up the street to the white gate. He kissed her again. "Should I come in with you, darling?"

She shook her head, smiling, and pressed his arm lightly before releasing him. He watched her go up the path to the house, between the dry bones of her mother's flowers. Her mussed appearance made him feel rather guilty, and her shameless acceptance of what had happened rather shocked him—he had expected tears and recriminations, if only as a matter of form. Yet he liked the honesty of her attitude, and he knew a sense of relief. He was committed now. He turned away toward Hill Street, feeling suddenly light and free, liberated from the weight of a decision that he had never allowed himself to consider openly.

5

■ On the porch behind him, Caroline Vail stood watching his receding figure until it swung out of sight on Hill Street. She was still smiling faintly. When he had disappeared, she drew a long breath and glanced at the lighted window beside her, that indicated that her mother, at least, would still be up and waiting for her. Automatically her hands went to her hair and she looked down at herself with some concern; then a bitter expression crossed her face, she let her hands fall and squared her shoulders defiantly, and turned toward the door, a general in a battle-stained uniform preparing to announce a victory.

A sound halted her and she looked quickly aside, as a man came around the corner of the porch. "Good evening, Miss Vail," George Menefee said, bowing with a flourish.

"What are you doing here?" she demanded, swinging about to face him. She looked at him sharply. "You've been at Morgan's again. You're drunk."

"Why not?" Menefee said, smiling. "A man has to do something to console himself when his girl goes strolling through the sagebrush with somebody else."

"I'm not your girl," she whispered. There was no conviction in the sound. "Leave me alone, hear? Go back to your saloon; that's where you belong. Don't come around here with your whiskey breath and your arrogant manner, Mr. George Menefee. Decent people don't want you around."

The man laughed softly. "Decent, Caroline?"

She followed the direction of his look and started to make some adjustment to her rumpled and damaged dress but stopped and drew herself up angrily. "I told you once: what I do is none of your business any longer, honey. You had your chance and you threw it away, over the tables at Morgan's."

"There'll be more money, darling. You'd be surprised at how many rich relatives I have back East, all of them in bad health."

"And none of them wanted you around, so they shipped you out here! And I don't want you around, either!"

"Don't you?" Menefee asked, reaching for her hand. She pulled away quickly. He laughed. "You see? You're afraid to let me touch you, even tonight, after being with him."

She said, "You'll never get out of this town, George. I know that now. You'll live here the rest of your life on your little pittance from the East and the few cases people throw you out of charity; and every time you get a few dollars you'll gamble them away. If—if I married you, that's all I'd have to look forward to: this miserable dirty little town and a drunken husband. Well, you can stay here,

George Menefee, but I'm not going to, hear? You promised once to take me back East with you—"

"Caroline, Caroline, do you want a man or a railroad ticket?" The man's voice was no longer playful and amused. Abruptly he reached for her and pulled her against him, overcoming her resistance without difficulty, since there was not, after the first flurry, a great deal of it to overcome. "You see?" he whispered at last, somewhat breathlessly. "We're two of a kind, darling."

"Because you made me—"

He laughed softly. "Made you, Caroline?"

She was crying now. "Let me go," she whispered. "Why can't you leave me alone?"

6

■ Ever since he had become well enough to put his life back on a normal schedule, John Parrish had taken his meals with the Rafter H crew, although this, of course, necessitated his getting up in the morning before the sky had more than turned pale behind the San Luis Hills. He had done this deliberately, as he had done many other things, so that they would not think he was putting on airs simply because he came from the East and happened to own the place. At first his presence had caused an awkward silence at the table; but gradually the men had become accustomed to seeing him there, and had even included him in their brief comments on the weather, the stock, the grass, and, occasionally, politics and women. Not that there was much conversation; these men came to the table to eat, not to talk.

The morning following his visit to town took the course

of all other mornings: Parrish seated himself at the end of the long table, made the good-morning noise that was expected of him, and began to eat from the well-filled plate the cook immediately put in front of him. The cook, a small, round, brown man with ropy black hair and a Spanish accent, had the theory that John Parrish had fallen ill simply because of the poor quality and inadequate quantity of Eastern food, and he had taken it upon himself to effect a cure in his own way.

Shortly after Parrish's arrival, Bud Hinkleman, the youngest member of the crew, stumbled in, late and only half awake as usual. Someone made the customary joke about sleeping sickness and everyone laughed. There was some regretful mention of Martin Coe's death. The return of Cole Hansen and his bride to Anchor was mentioned.

Seated at the end of the table, eating the second helping put before him by the cook, Parrish watched and listened and kept his silence, as was his custom. He was not one of these men, and everyone in the kitchen knew it; they tolerated him and they took his pay, but they had by no means accepted him. It was significant, he thought, that he was not asked to describe the sheriff's killing; they knew he had been present and doubtless felt he should have done something to prevent it. They had never been quite happy, he knew, about working for a man who did not wear a gun.

As he watched them eating and talking briefly among themselves, it occurred to Parrish, by no means for the first time, just how tough this group of riders would look to the people he had known back East; they were a hard-bitten bunch by city standards. And there was no doubt that they lived up to their appearance; even Bud Hinkleman, well under twenty, had shown no hesitation at all about using his fists, his knees, and his boots, when one of the others had goaded him into losing his temper. It had been a savage fight, which the older man had not won easily. The others were older and more experienced than the boy, and they made a fine crew. Yet, looking at them now, Parrish was aware that there was a difference between these men and those he had seen riding for Anchor, just as there was a difference between a raw recruit and a finished soldier. These were undoubtedly brave men, but their job was cattle. They carried guns by force of habit, but their real tools were the rope and branding iron.

Jim McCloud, the foreman, had finished his coffee; now he dried his mustache, pushed his chair back slightly, and leaned back to roll a cigarette. It was a recognized signal, and those who had not yet finished increased the pace of their eating.

"Harry," McCloud said to the man sitting next to him, "you take the river north from where you left it yesterday. When you hit Boundary Creek, swing east. Haze back any Anchor beef that's drifted across, but stay out of trouble with their riders, hear?" McCloud turned to Bud Hinkleman. "Bud, you're packing your gear up to Nelly's Canyon and relieving Wash Breed. Take a week's grub up to the line cabin with you. Jackson, you and DeRosa. . . ."

Parrish finished his coffee slowly. This part of the morning always embarrassed him slightly by reminding him that he still had only a superficial knowledge of what was involved in running a cattle ranch. He had been lucky, he reflected, in finding Jim McCloud still here when he arrived, and in having sense enough to prevail on the man to stay on. As Walter Hard's foreman, McCloud had barely managed to keep the ranch going on what little money Hard could spare from his drinking; given a free hand by Parrish, and cash to work with, he had in three years developed the place to where it was returning an excellent profit on Parrish's original investment.

He was a stringy man of medium height whose black hair was interspersed with gray, giving a pepper-and-salt effect, not only to his hair, but to his eyebrows and thick mustache as well. He had a curious, unswerving loyalty to the ranch that employed him that seemed to have little to do with personalities; he had accepted Parrish's illness as he had, apparently, accepted Walter Hard's drinking. Only a growing meagerness of his face and body betrayed his age, which was considerable.

Having given his instructions for the day, he rose, and the rest of the men followed his lead. Parrish spoke quickly, before they could leave the kitchen.

"Just a minute."

They turned to look at him, a little surprised, since he had made it a habit not to interfere in the running of the ranch.

"What is it, Mr. Parrish?" McCloud asked.

Parrish said, "You've got a right to know this, all of you. I am selling this ranch and going back East."

There was a small pause; then McCloud asked slowly, "Do you have a buyer in mind, Mr. Parrish?"

"Mr. Wilkison sent a message to town asking me to ride over and talk business with him today. I can think of no other business we'd have to discuss."

"You'd sell to Anchor?" There was a faint edge to the foreman's voice.

Parrish said, "Jim, don't try to involve me in your local feuds. I know your former employer had a fight with Wilkison; and perhaps you share his feelings, and I'm sorry about that. I don't approve of some aspects of the situation here, myself. But the way things are going only confirms my judgment that it's time for me to get out of here before I get involved in quarrels that have nothing to do with me." He looked at all of them for a moment and went on: "I mentioned it only because you've all got a right to know what to expect; also because I want to make sure that nobody runs any risks for me or Rafter H out of a mistaken sense of loyalty. Things are getting a little strained around here, and we all know it, and it may take some time for me to get my affairs straightened out. In the meantime I want every man working for this ranch to mind his business and watch his step. I want no fighting or shooting, regardless of the provocation, do you understand? In fact, you have my explicit orders to run like hell at the first sign of trouble, even if it should involve Rafter H property. Is that perfectly clear? I don't want any heroes on the payroll. I may not be much of a cattleman, but so far nobody's been hurt working for me, and I want to keep it that way for the remainder of my stay out here."

He went out of the kitchen, closing the door behind him. In the living-room, he stood for a moment irresolute, looking about him idly; this was a rough room mainly given over to the business of the ranch, and a scarred old desk in the corner held the ranch accounts. A heavy, round table held a lamp that needed cleaning; there were a few large chairs, a rack of rifles of assorted makes and calibers, and a threadbare Indian rug on the floor. The magazines and books Parrish had accumulated during his illness were stacked in dusty piles beyond the fireplace.

He frowned at the room, trying to fit into it the small, bright presence of Caroline Vail, and failing; she was right in not wanting to come here to live, he thought. It would take a different kind of woman to make a home of this place; which, he told himself hastily, was not necessarily a reflection on Caroline. He did not, after all, belong here, either; although he could not honestly say that he had found his stay here unpleasant; in fact, he had enjoyed it. . . . He grimaced at his own efforts, now that she had come into his mind, to keep his thoughts away from certain vivid and recent memories associated with Caroline. Parrish was still a little shocked at both of them for behaving as they had. Although he had begun to suspect himself of being capable of it—three years was a long time for a man to maintain a proper and restrained and decorous courtship—he had not really guessed it of her despite the occasional hints of her nature that he had received; and he could not help being disconcerted as well as wryly amused by the pretty skill with which she had provoked and used the disturbing incident.

Yet he was not hypocrite enough to try to tell himself that she had tricked him into acting in a manner entirely foreign to his nature; nor could he convince himself that he regretted what had happened, particularly since she had shown no signs of regret. It did occur to him, however, that the marriage upon which he was embarking was going to differ, in some respects, from the respectable picture of wedded bliss that he had, somewhat vaguely, anticipated.

The sound of horsemen entering the yard brought him out of his thoughts, and McCloud opened the front door.

"It's Silas Purdue and a couple of his boys, Captain,"

the foreman said. It was his habit to use the military title in public, although Parrish had pointed out that he was no longer entitled to it.

"What do they want?"

"Well," McCloud said judiciously, "I couldn't rightly say, but from the looks of him I'd guess that old Silas was mad about something."

Parrish sighed, found his hat, and joined the older man. They crossed the porch together and descended the dusty path; the Rafter H ranch house was built on a small knoll overlooking the surrounding country. The men from Box Seven had not dismounted. Silas Purdue urged his horse forward a step as Parrish and McCloud drew near. Looking up at him, Parrish noticed how all these men seemed to be of an age: Jim McCloud and Silas Purdue, and Walter Hard who had drunk himself to death, and Jack Mahoney who had been forced to flee the valley, and Martin Coe who had been killed. They had all, apparently, crossed the plains and come into the Basin within a few years of each other, at almost the same time of life.

Silas Purdue had sparse gray hair and a long New England face that the sun had turned red instead of brown. His clothes and his gear were old and worn, as was the horse upon which he sat: a bony white animal with an ugly head. He carried a rifle in a saddle scabbard, and the two men with him were also armed.

"Light down and have some coffee, Mr. Purdue," Parrish said, regarding this man from the ground.

"I did not come here to be social," Silas Purdue said grimly. "Is it true that you're considering selling this ranch to Wilkison?"

"To anyone who will pay a reasonable price," Parrish said.

The man above him said, "We have been good neighbors to you, John Parrish. The first winter you were here, my wife helped nurse you when you were close to death."

"I would be glad to sell the place to you, Mr. Purdue."

Silas Purdue made a snorting sound. "If I had that kind of money, I would have bought Jack Mahoney's place rather than let that crippled old vulture have it."

45

Parrish said, speaking rather stiffly, "I'll always be grateful for your kindness, and that of Mrs. Purdue. But I don't think that if you can't make me an offer you have a right to object to my listening to those who can."

The older man leaned forward in his saddle. "Listen to me, young man. Twelve years ago, Lew Wilkison's riders killed my boy. He was doing them no harm; he was not even trespassing on what could by any stretch of the imagination be called Anchor range, but they beat him up so badly that he died in his mother's arms after reaching home. It was their way of teaching us smaller ranchers to be respectful to Anchor. I have fought Lew Wilkison ever since, and I will continue to fight him until I am dead. I consider no man a friend who will have dealings with him. So keep off Box Seven from now on, John Parrish. You are not welcome there!"

Silas Purdue reined the ugly white horse about; then abruptly swung it back again. "One more thing, boy. There are two kinds of people we don't like out here. There's the fellow with a plow who guts the range to raise a couple of crops and moves on leaving a place nothing but thistles will grow on. And then there's the gentleman from the East who buys himself a ranch to turn a quick profit, little caring what happens to the country after he leaves. Of the two, we prefer the nester. At least he does some honest work with his hands!"

7

■ Shortly before lunch a man named Kruger, on his way home to his own small spread back in the San Luis Hills, stopped by with the news that a man named Magruder had been appointed acting sheriff.

"Magruder?" McCloud said. "Dark, heavy-set fellow? Used to work for Anchor before a horse rolled on him?"

"Yeh," Kruger said. He drained his cup of coffee and rose. "That's the man. Well, I'll be riding along. Much obliged."

"Stay and eat," Parrish said.

Kruger shook his head. "I thank you, but the family will be expecting me." He made a lean shape, framed in the open doorway, a rangy man with light hair shaggy about his neck and ears, who was called Tex by all who knew him. Parrish had of him the kind of information he had of all his neighbors: Kruger had a pretty, dark-haired wife and a little blond daughter, and he ran his small place with the aid of one Mexican rider who appeared in town regularly, once a month, and was drunk for three days. Tex Kruger was well liked and reported to be honest.

There was clearly a question in this tall man's mind now as he stood in the doorway preparing to take his leave, and he said without inflection, "Martin Coe was a good man. The Basin won't be the same without him."

"For a fact," McCloud said.

Kruger said in the same idle voice, "I hear Cole Hansen was telling somebody before his wedding that as soon as he took over at Anchor there'd be some changes made, like cleaning all the rustlers out of the San Loos. Some people seem to figure anybody runs less cattle than they do is bound to be a rustler."

Sensing where this was leading—the man was looking directly at him—Parrish said carefully, "Maybe you should have a talk with Silas Purdue. He seems to share your feeling about Anchor."

Tex Kruger turned his head and spat deliberately over the edge of the porch behind him. "It is the one thing Mr. Purdue and us Hills folks have in common, I reckon. There have been a few disagreements in the past, Box Seven being back in the foothills like it is, and cattle having a habit of straying the way they do. Besides, Silas Purdue is a man who kills his own snakes. It's an attitude us smaller folk can admire, without being able to afford it." He hesi-

47

tated. "Well, you might keep in mind that there's men who can ride and shoot all through the Hills. They are willing to fight for the privilege of being left alone."

Parrish said, "I'm afraid you've come to the wrong place. As a matter of fact, I'm riding over to Anchor on business right after lunch."

"I see." The Texan creased his hat carefully and placed it on his head. "Well, that kind of answers my question, I reckon. Much obliged for the coffee." He paused at the edge of the porch and looked back. "They tell me you served with Kirkpatrick in Georgia, Captain."

Parrish said, "That's true. We were under Kirkpatrick's command in that campaign."

"That's funny." Kruger did not smile. "From over on our side, we got the idea Kirkpatrick had a pretty tough bunch of boys. But I reckon they always look tougher coming at you than running away."

Then he was gone down the path. Parrish stepped forward and watched him mount his horse in an effortless manner and ride off without looking back. Parrish glanced at McCloud, who was careful not to meet his eyes. *Forget it,* he told himself, *forget it; you're not a boy, to be influenced by somebody's calling you a coward. You know more about your courage than he does. It is still no fight of yours.*

After lunch, he walked down the hill with the foreman, facing into the hot wind that had come up from the south. He glanced at the gray gelding that had been saddled for him, and frowned at a thing that displeased him. The incidents of the morning had rubbed his temper raw and he was glad to find an issue he could meet squarely.

"Take it off," he said.

McCloud said, "Now, Captain—"

Parrish said, "Damn it, Jim, I'm not a captain. I'm just a poor damn civilian trying to get rid of a piece of property that belongs to me." He swung about to look at the dark and lanky rider who had brought the gelding around. The horse itself was a subtle insult, being quite old enough to have ridden through Georgia with Sherman's army; it was the mount that had been selected for him, for gentleness, when he had first been declared well enough to ride. The childishness of the gesture, once he realized it, saved him from losing his temper completely. He spoke quietly to the dark rider, whose name was Joe DeRosa. "Take it off, Joe. I'm not riding to Anchor with a rifle on my saddle. That's asking for trouble, isn't it, when I'm known not to pack a gun?"

He watched DeRosa remove carbine and scabbard, then swung himself into the saddle and looked down at them, and at the ranch house and outbuildings. It was a bleak enough place; yet he knew a faint stirring of regret. To hide it he wheeled the gray around sharply.

"Don't expect me for dinner; I'll be riding into town afterward and I may stay overnight."

There seemed to be no more to say. He kicked the horse into motion, aware, as always, that his straight-backed, cavalryman's way of riding seemed peculiar to these men; which was not reason enough to change, particularly now that he was about to take his leave of them. What they thought of him was a matter of no great importance; they would forget him, and a year from now he would not remember their names. The important thing, now, was to extricate himself from all of this without losing his temper or allowing himself to be goaded or bullied or ridiculed into becoming involved.

He set off northward at a steady pace. Crossing Hard Creek at the customary ford a mile above the ranch, he climbed out of the wide and deep arroyo through which the stream ran—low at this time of year—and reined in briefly at the top to let the gelding blow. Then he followed the plainly marked trail through the rougher country beyond, which occasionally lifted him high enough for a view of the entire Basin. The full sight of this broad, broken valley between two mountain ranges never failed to stir him; but today he did not pause, as he usually did, to pick out the landmarks with which he had become acquainted during his stay here. He would not need them again.

Presently he splashed through the shallow waters of Boundary Creek and was on Anchor range. He swung westward then, through country that was quite new to him, some time later fording the swift and cold waters of the Big Gun River at a riffle. It was still a long ride to his destination from this point, and the afternoon was drawing to a close when he drew up at last on a rise of land and, looking to the northwest, saw the buildings of Anchor before him. It pleased him to have struck them squarely; he still, apparently, had not lost the knack of finding his way over unfamiliar terrain.

He studied the big ranch thoughtfully, seeing it for the first time although he had lived within half a day's ride of it for three years. His approach had not gone unnoticed; a man had followed him for several miles and was now watching him from a little way back down the ridge, making no great attempt at concealment. Parrish paid him no attention, but continued to regard the buildings ahead with interest. Even at a distance, the house Lew Wilkison had built for his Spanish bride made its impression well. It was a great, sprawling place with white columns.

Parrish frowned and found himself thinking idly that, lying in a gentle hollow as it did, surrounded by trees and flanked by the cottonwoods of some creek, this was a pleasant, sheltered, and attractive spot, but one that should be easy to surprise, militarily speaking. Clearly Lew Wilkison had been too assured of his own strength and of the power of his reputation to make any sacrifices of appearance or comfort for the sake of making his fine house defensible. Parrish put the notion aside; it was high time, he told himself, that he stopped thinking like a soldier.

No one came out to greet him as he rode up, but he was aware of two men lounging in apparent idleness near the corner of the house. He slid stiffly to the ground, gave the reins a turn about the rail, and moved back to ease the girths of the double-cinched Texas saddle, which still seemed to him a lot of rig to put on a horse, even if it made a comfortable seat for the rider. He was busy with this, pushing his head into the gray's flank to keep the animal from moving into him, when a rider came up at a gallop and pulled up sharply.

"Do you call that a horse?" Judith Wilkison's voice asked lightly.

Finished with his job, Parrish looked up and watched her swing out of the saddle, the grace of the movement broken as she had to pause briefly to free the hem of the full, divided riding-skirt she was wearing.

"This damn skirt!" she said irritably, reaching the ground. "Well, if Dad and Martha had their way, I'd be riding side-saddle, which is a fool way to sit a horse if I ever saw one. . . . But really, Mr. Parrish, can't you find anything better than that to ride around your ranch?"

She looked critically at the gray, which looked even less beautiful than usual, contrasted with the glossy chestnut gelding beside it.

Parrish patted his mount's neck. "You'll hurt Smoky's feelings, Miss Wilkison. Why, this is what my men picked out for me to ride today. They don't seem to have a very high opinion of me for coming here. But we get along very well, Smoky and I. People don't expect much of either of us, and they generally get just about what they expect."

He had intended the mock humility as a joke; to his surprise, Judith Wilkison seemed to take him seriously. She frowned, slapping at her skirt with the riding-crop she carried, as she studied him. He noticed that she was wearing a plain white shirtwaist that seemed to emphasize the pleasant if unfashionably boyish tan of her skin; the simple costume was a great deal more becoming to her than the elaborate dress she had worn in town the previous day. He realized that she was really quite an attractive young girl despite her height, almost equal to his. It was a pity that nobody seemed to have bothered to teach her manners.

She said, "We've had dudes in this country before, Mr. Parrish. All kinds of dudes. But I can't recall ever seeing one like you before. Honest, you have me puzzled."

Parrish said dryly, "I assure you, it's unintentional."

"I'm not certain I believe that," Judith Wilkison said with rather surprising bluntness. "I have a hunch very few things you do are unintentional, like leaving off your gun, for instance. You must know how to shoot; you were in the army. So why set yourself apart from everybody else

51

by going unarmed? There's a reason, isn't there? You're a little too good to be true, Mr. Parrish. You're so modest about your military record, so brave about your illness. . . . I don't think I trust you one damn bit. Not that it matters, since you're leaving us, anyway."

This was direct talk, and it took him aback; they did not know each other well enough to indulge in personalities like this. It was clear that Judith Wilkison had been giving him some thought since she had seen him yesterday; for some reason, the idea was a disturbing one.

"I think I'm entitled to an explanation," Parrish said.

She nodded. "Most dudes that come out here, Mr. Parrish, can hardly wait to get off the stage before dolling themselves up in a great big white hat and a shirt you can see three counties away on a dusty day. Then they buy themselves a pair of hand-carved boots, some woolly chaps that are about as much use in this country as a third stirrup, and a pair of Mexican spurs with rowels the size of doughnuts. They hang one or maybe even two Colt guns about them and climb on the biggest and blackest horse they can find. If they live through the first thirty seconds they figure they've got the country licked; by God, they're cowboys, and nobody's going to tell them different. In fact, nobody's going to tell them anything. . . . Well, the Basin's been waiting for three years for you to break out with the symptoms, Mr. Parrish, and nothing's happened. Some people, I think, are even ready to give up and admit that you might possibly be human, even if you did come from the East and don't wear a gun. At least they were until today; now, I don't know."

"But not you, Miss Wilkison?" Parrish asked.

She said quietly, "I'm not sure. There's a kind of man who knows how to act natural any place he happens to be; who just kind of falls into the ways people around him, or makes them like his ways. But there's also a kind of man who can get along anywhere just by being clever and careful." She gave him a quick glance. "I'm afraid I don't like clever and careful people, Mr. Parrish."

"I will keep it in mind," he murmured.

"I think you will," she agreed. "I think you keep a good

many things in that mind of yours, Mr. Parrish; and I think it's probably a very good mind. I'm sure you'll find plenty of opportunities for using it, back East."

He said softly, "You're trying to pick a fight with me. Why?"

She said, "Go inside, Mr. Parrish. They're waiting for you. I think they'll go as high as five thousand if you handle it right."

"They'll have to go higher than that."

"Will they? They got the Mahoney place for three."

Parrish, rather bewildered, said, "This is your father and brother-in-law we're discussing now?"

Judith Wilkison said, "My father is an old man, Mr. Parrish. He's had a long time to sit in his wheelchair and hate the people who deprived him of the use of his legs. I don't blame my father. But I do blame those who'd take advantage of his bitterness; and I also blame those who encourage him by making no resistance to the grandiose schemes that have been put into his head!" She drew a long breath and laughed sharply. "I don't suppose I really have any right to be disappointed in you, Mr. Parrish. There's no reason why you should be interested in trying to show Dad that most of the people he hates are gone now, and that others are coming in who are willing to try to get along with us on a basis of mutual respect. . . . But it's not your fight, is it, Mr. Parrish? This country has given you your health and, I suppose, a financial profit. What happens to it now is no concern of yours."

Parrish looked at her face, flushed with the vehemence with which she had spoken. He said in a very dry voice, "It must be fun arranging battles for other people to fight, Miss Wilkison."

She glanced at him quickly, and more color flooded her face beneath the golden tan of her skin. Suddenly she looked very young indeed, despite her tallness and the severity of her riding costume.

"I didn't mean it like that," she said after a moment. "I just meant. . . . Well, damn it, you can't blame me for wanting to see *somebody* show up that man for the cold and ruthless fortune-hunter that he is. How Martha can

53

stand—" She checked herself abruptly. "But you're not interested in our private affairs, Mr. Parrish. I'm sorry to have delayed you. I think Dad and Cole are waiting for you in the study."

8

■ After she had left him, Parrish remained for a moment longer by the horses, brushing the dust from his clothes and putting his thoughts in order, before starting for the house. He found himself noting the details of the ranch as he stood there; unlike Rafter H, where a visitor made his approach to the house through the dust of the yard, Anchor hid its outbuildings to the rear of the main dwelling, while the front boasted a circular drive beneath the trees, and even as much grass as could be expected to grow in this semi-desert climate. It was a prosperous and well-tended establishment that bore little resemblance to his vague notions of Anchor as a grim and fortified robber's-roost of a place.

He became aware of a slender, dark-haired, feminine figure watching him from the big veranda. He had no idea how long this girl had been standing there, and her silent presence gave him an unpleasant feeling of having been spied upon. He recognized her at once, of course, having seen her several times at a distance. She was not someone a man forgot.

"Good afternoon, Mrs. Hansen," he said, removing his hat as he went forward.

She did not speak, waiting for him to reach her. Approaching, he could not help being struck by the marked difference between this sister and the tall girl in riding clothes who had just left him. Lew Wilkison's older daughter was wearing a summery dress of some light figured material; her almost black hair was drawn back from her face to be gathered up smoothly at the nape of her neck in the Spanish fashion.

She was extremely beautiful, and Parrish's mind admitted this readily; nevertheless, as he reached her side, he was conscious of a feeling of disappointment. This was a bride of only a few days, a girl who had just returned from her honeymoon; but there was in her none of the look of awakening that often transfigured the plainest women at this moment of their lives. Martha Hansen looked as cool and serene, Parrish reflected, as if she had spent the past month in a convent. It was no way for a bride to look.

"We have been waiting for you, Captain Parrish," she said, picking up her skirts to precede him into the house. He saw no reason to apologize, since no specific time had been set for his visit, and he did not speak. "Please close the door," Martha Hansen said when they were inside. "This wind brings so much dust into the house, it's like living in a tent. . . . What did my little sister have to say to you, Captain Parrish?"

Her amused, light voice, dwelling on the adjective, made a joke of the younger girl's tallness; it reduced Judith, by implication, to the status of an overgrown child. Yet Parrish thought he could detect a faint undertone of disquiet that made him glance sharply at his attractive companion as they walked along the hall together.

He said, "I found it difficult to make out precisely what she wanted to say, Mrs. Hansen. She expressed an unfavorable opinion of my horse, and I gathered she wasn't greatly impressed by me, either. Altogether, she seemed in a rather hostile mood."

Martha Hansen laughed. "I'm afraid you'll have to make allowances for Judy, Captain. My little sister has always been a problem; she's a wild and irresponsible person in many ways. She thinks nothing of disappearing for days at a time, coming back dreadfully dirty and ragged and quite unconcerned about the fact that Dad and I have

55

been worrying ourselves sick about her. I haven't been able to make her understand that language and behavior that might be permissible in a boy are hardly proper for a young lady; and she seems to take no interest in the things I try to teach her." Martha Hansen shook her head and smiled sadly. "She won't even listen to me politely any longer. I'm afraid it's a rather difficult time for Judy, Mr. Parrish, and I hope you'll make allowances for her."

They had stopped in front of a closed door. "Why difficult?" Parrish asked.

"Why, as her older sister, I've always done my best to take the place of her mother," the dark-haired girl said serenely. "But of course now that I'm married—well, I'm afraid Judy's somewhat jealous of my husband's claims on my attention. But, heavens, you're not interested in our family problems, Captain Parrish! I just wanted to apologize for my sister's rudeness." She turned crisply to face the door, and when he opened it for her she swept past him and into the study beyond, a small, businesslike, masculine room that apparently served as an office for ranch affairs.

Of the two men inside, the older was the more striking, and it was toward him that Parrish looked first. Lew Wilkison had been a legendary, unseen character for so long that Parrish could not, for a moment, reconcile everything he had heard in the past three years with the sight of the great crippled figure that confronted him from the wheelchair pulled up alongside the desk. Somehow, in the stories, Wilkison had seemed ageless; but this was an old man, as Judith had said. The great bones were still there, but the exercise of maneuvering the wheelchair had not been enough to keep up the muscles of shoulders, chest, and arms against the encroachments of the years; and the legs, of course, were wasted sticks beneath the blanket that covered them. The great shock of white hair and the bristling white mustache made a startling contrast to the broad red face that was the only part of the man that seemed to retain vigor and even a kind of grim fierceness.

"So you're Parrish," Wilkison shouted. "My daughter Judith said you looked like a polite little boy with red hair and freckles. Damn if she wasn't right."

"Dad," Martha said, "Captian Parrish is right in the room. He can hear you perfectly well."

"Captain, eh?" the old man bellowed. "What were you captain of, a nursery? Ah, come on in, boy; don't mind me. Help yourself to something to drink if you like. Over there." He waved a hand at a table by the window.

"No, thank you," Parrish said.

"Why not? You're old enough, aren't you?"

Parrish said, "Dr. Kinsman discourages my drinking. I'm still under his orders."

Wilkison studied him for a moment, and there was a sudden shrewdness to the fierce blue eyes. "You're a liar, son," he said in a quite normal voice. "Spit it out. What's wrong with Anchor liquor?"

Parrish said deliberately, "Seeing Sheriff Coe shot in the back spoiled my taste for it, Mr. Wilkison."

The old man's bony hands gripped the arms of the chair as if in an effort to help him rise. "Why, you young—!" After a moment, surprisingly, Wilkison grinned. "Damn, I should have known you didn't have red hair for nothing, boy. Will you drink with me if I tell you I'm sorry as hell about Martin, and that the yellow pup that shot him has been booted off this ranch? Why, Martin was a friend of mine; we came to this country together. We had our disagreements, sure, particularly after he got old and cranky and started standing up for every rustler and shirt-tail farmer in the country; rub Martin the wrong way and he'd stand up for anybody, and I reckon I didn't put it to him right when I tried to show him how a big outfit like Anchor's entitled to a little extra protection from the law, since everybody figures they're fair game. . . . Ah, hell, I miss Martin, boy. If it had ever come to the point where I figured he needed shooting, I'd have had myself rolled out on Front Street and done the job myself. You can't hold it against me because one rat happened to get on the payroll; I tell you, I kicked that fancy little two-gun pipsqueak out of here so fast his tail's still burning." Wilkison swung his head toward the man sitting behind the desk. "Cole, pour this boy a drink, damn it."

After a moment, Cole Hansen rose in silence and, presently, Parrish took the glass that was offered him; he had made his point, and there was nothing to be gained by carrying the matter further. Martha Hansen had left the room. He found a chair facing the desk; it was low and put him at a disadvantage that he knew was deliberate. He lifted his glass to the old man and tasted the excellent whisky it contained. Wilkison finished his in one draft, Hansen took a deep drink and set his glass on the desk.

There followed a moment of silence to indicate that the social amenities had been concluded and it was time for business. Parrish used the pause to study Cole Hansen carefully. He knew the former Anchor foreman better, perhaps, than he knew anyone else from the big ranch; they had met in town and on the range during roundup time. Nevertheless he had no feeling of understanding the man. Sitting behind the desk, Lew Wilkison's new son-in-law had the same misplaced look that always characterized Jim McCloud at the desk at Rafter H: an outdoors man never looked quite right behind a desk. Hansen was a big man in every respect, almost a heavy one, yet he knew how to handle himself lightly. Even in a chair he seemed to maintain full control of himself, making a point, apparently, of not letting himself sag into the shape of the furniture that supported him, as if there was a driving force inside him that would not let him relax.

He had a long, tanned, clean-shaven face, much darker than the yellow mane of his hair. His nose had been broken at some time; the bridge of it was slightly thickened and not quite straight. He carried a small scar on one cheekbone, another near the corner of his mouth, and a longer one made a faint light line that followed the jawbone back almost two inches from the point of his chin. In the side of his neck there was a dimple that could have been made by nothing but a bullet. Reading the signs that life had left upon this big man, not more than a year or two older than himself, Parrish knew a feeling of respect. This was, he knew, a larger, tougher, and more experienced man than John Parrish; this was, undoubtedly, a brave man and a dangerous adversary; an ambitious man with no visible weaknesses except, perhaps, a certain arrogance that might lead him to underestimate the abilities of other men, particularly those smaller than himself.

Mr. Wilkison broke the silence. "Well, I hear you're planning to sell and go back East, Parrish. The climate's got your lungs all fixed up, eh? I wish it would do the same for my legs."

Parrish said, "Well, I'm considering selling, yes, if I can get a fair price. If not, I'll just hang onto the place as an investment, I suppose."

Hansen spoke for the first time: "How much do you want?"

Unlike Wilkison, who still seemed cordial enough, Hansen put his question in a curt and hostile manner. Parrish glanced at him and was a little taken aback to see a gun in the big man's hands. Hansen was toying with the weapon, idly shaking the cartridges out of it, one by one, onto the papers on the desk.

Lew Wilkison laughed. "All right, boys, go to it," he said, "Nothing I like to watch more than a good horse trade. Cole, you watch out for this here city feller, or he'll trim you."

Hansen did not smile. "How much do you want?" he repeated, watching Parrish coldly.

"How much are you willing to pay?" Parrish countered.

"You're low on stock this year and most of what you've got is pretty scrubby stuff," Hansen said. "And the buildings and improvements aren't worth much to us; all we're interested in is the range rights."

Parrish said dryly, "Yes, it's a mighty poor place. It's a wonder Mr. Wilkison even bothered to ask me to come here today. I guess he wanted to do me a favor."

Still unsmiling, Hansen said, "I still haven't heard your asking price, Parrish."

Parrish said, "You probably know what I paid Walter Hard for the place; that's no secret. I want to get my money out, no more."

Hansen gave a perfunctory laugh. "Old Walter played you for a sucker, fellow. You must know that by this time. You can't expect Anchor to pay for your mistakes."

Lew Wilkison chuckled, watching them. The old man had swung his wheelchair around and backed it off a little so that he could see them both, and his blue eyes were alive with malicious pleasure.

"Go on, boys, go on," he said. "You're doing fine."

Parrish paid no attention to him but kept his eyes on Hansen. Having emptied his gun once, and reloaded it, the big man now began to shake the lead-tipped shells out of it a second time. He handled the weapon, Parrish thought, with the casual familiarity with which a confirmed pipe smoker would manipulate his pipe. The revolver held Parrish's interest also. Not only were metallic-cartridge weapons still something of a novelty to him—only a few had been available during the war—but this one had a striking peculiarity that would catch the attention of anyone at all accustomed to firearms: it lacked a trigger. It had clearly been altered, gunman fashion, for thumbing or fanning the hammer; and the fact that he would possess such a weapon threw a new light on the character of Cole Hansen, indicating that he might be something more—or less —than just an ambitious range boss who had been smart enough, or lucky enough, to marry his employer's daughter.

"Well," Parrish said deliberately, "if that's your attitude, Hansen, and if Mr. Wilkison concurs in it, I guess I've had my ride for nothing. The price I paid for Rafter H was a fair one—I may not be much of a cattleman but I have some notion of business—and I have no intention of letting the place go for a lower figure. There's no necessity for it, since I have no immediate need for the money; I've still got an interest in a firm back East that will pay me a reasonable living. I have a good foreman and a good crew; they can work the ranch without me until I find a buyer who'll meet my price."

"They might work it for you," Hansen said softly. "But will they fight it for you?"

There was a brief silence. The big, blond man behind the desk swept up the five shells in front of him and, without glancing down, fed them all back into the chambers of the cylinder so rapidly that it looked like a conjuring

60

trick. He spun the cylinder to place the empty under the hammer, shoved the weapon away into the holster at his side, and stood up abruptly; but it was Lew Wilkison who spoke, forestalling whatever his son-in-law had been about to say.

"Take it easy, Cole. There's no need to get tough, yet." The old man swung his wheelchair toward Parrish. "Let's put the cards on the table, boy. Look at it this way: Anchor needs grass. Down south of us is range we can use, range we need, kept from us just because I once gave a bunch of stubborn old men cause to hate my guts. They've been holding a line across the Basin for twelve years; every time a man would die or move away, the rest would take over his range, even though they didn't need it and weren't going to use it. They'd even let nesters squat on it and plow it to hell rather than let Anchor get it. Well, I'm plumb out of patience with this orneriness, Parrish. I've got the Peterson and Mahoney places now, and I'm taking the rest. I'm an old man myself, and half of me's dead and useless, but there's a man in the family now who isn't tied to a goddam wheelchair, and he's going to do the job for me, eh, Cole?" Wilkison cleared his throat and went on. "So don't let's hear any more foolishness about keeping that ranch of yours for an investment, son. You're selling out, boy. One way or another, you're selling out. To us."

Parrish studied the old man's wide, red face for a certain length of time. *Take it easy, now,* he warned himself. *Take this home and look it over; to blurt out what you're thinking will do no good. Give yourself time.* He drained the remaining contents of his glass, set the glass aside, took his hat from the arm of his chair, and rose. The two men facing him watched him closely.

He said quietly, "There are two questions I'd like to ask, Mr. Wilkison."

"Go ahead, son."

"Why didn't you buy the place from Walter Hard, when he was selling, three years ago? Instead of letting me have it."

"Walter wouldn't have sold to Anchor. He'd have given the place to Silas Purdue first."

Parrish said, "Mr. Hard was a drunkard, and sick. He died not very much later, I understand. Even at the time, he could hardly see to sign his name. You could have bought through someone he didn't know, a dummy. He'd never have guessed the trick." The old man did not speak, but grinned at him pleasantly. Parrish said dryly, "I see. I was the dummy."

"Something like that, I reckon. Besides, the time wasn't right; Jack Mahoney was still acting stubborn, and Cole wasn't part of the family yet. I'm good at waiting, boy."

Parrish nodded slowly. "All right. That's one question. Now, just how high are you willing to go?"

Wilkison said, without looking aside, "What was that figure we settled on, Cole?"

"Four thousand," Cole Hansen said.

"That isn't even a good down payment," Parrish murmured. "The stock alone is worth—"

"We don't figure that way," the yellow-haired man said softly. "We don't figure what the place is worth, fellow. We just figure what it's worth to us to get you off without a fight. There's our offer. You've got twenty-four hours to think it over."

9

■ From the window of her bedroom on the second floor—now no longer hers alone—Martha Hansen watched the visitor ride off; something about the manner in which he controlled his obvious anger, neither jerking the gray horse around nor spurring it away, made her frown thoughtfully. She stood there for a moment longer and was about to turn away when the door of the room opened. She checked herself and continued to look out the window as if unaware of the man beside her, until he reached her.

"Well?" she said then.

"He walked out mad. But he'll be back."

"Don't be too sure, Cole. How much did you offer?"

"Four thousand."

"I thought we said more."

"He was cocky. He wouldn't drink our liquor, at first, because of what happened in town yesterday. He needed to be taught a lesson. He'll be back."

She said, "Why bother to teach lessons to a man you're never going to see again, Cole? For six thousand you could have had the place; that girl of his in town wouldn't have let him turn it down. She has big-city ideas. But four is a slap in the face. . . . What did Dad say when he refused a drink?"

"The old man apologized to the squirt. Said he was sorry and— Damn it, Martha, look at a man when you talk to him!" He reached for her abruptly and swung her around. She was passive and non-resistant in his hands. He swore and released her. "Damn it, aren't you ever going to forget—?"

"Is it something you'd expect a woman to forget, Cole?"

"I was a little rough, maybe; and what with the wedding I had been drinking some—"

"You were disgusting, Cole; and if you ever act like that toward me again, I'll leave you. When you come into this room I expect you to forget the manners you learned from whores and dancehall women. Either that, or go back to them with my blessing. We made a bargain, Cole, but I don't consider that being mauled in a drunken fashion and having—having my clothes torn and my—my body pounded black and blue—" A faint color came into her face. "That's no part of the bargain, Cole, and I won't stand for it. If it ever happens again—"

He smiled slowly. "If it ever happens again, honey, you'll like it like you did the first time."

She stared at him for a moment. Abruptly she swung a hand sharply across his face and turned away from him.

The sound of the blow seemed to hang in the room for measurable seconds.

Cole Hansen chuckled. "You're learning, honey. . . . No, I'm not going to touch you. You're safe as in church. I can wait for some of that ice to melt. We both know you're human beneath it, don't we, honey? That's our little secret, yours and mine." He swung away. "I have work to do; I'll see you at dinner."

"Cole."

Her voice, matter of fact now, checked him at the door. He looked back. "What is it?"

"Be careful, Cole. I can take things from a successful man that I would not tolerate from a failure."

"Failure?" He laughed. "Honey, I promised you the governor's mansion, and I keep my promises. What's troubling you?"

She said, "I don't trust a red-haired man who can keep his temper. It's unnatural."

"That baby-faced punk? Why, he doesn't even wear a gun; that's how badly he wants to stay out of trouble."

"He's about thirty years old. That would make him only a little over twenty when the war ended. Cole, they didn't make twenty-year-old boys captain in the cavalry for nothing."

Hansen frowned. "It's a thought, honey. I'll keep it in mind. Maybe a little more pressure is what the lad needs. Thanks for the warning."

When he had gone, his wife moved slowly from the window to the door and stood there for a moment as if listening for his return.

Hearing no sound, she turned to the near-by wardrobe to select a dress for dinner. As she made her choice, deliberating over each gown for a moment before passing on to the next, there was on her lips a small, secret smile of which she herself was not aware.

10

■ Rafter H range looked unfamiliar in the dark; Parrish had never crossed it alone before except in daylight. He missed the vague trail below Boundary Creek, cut east to pick it up and failed, gave up, and headed southeast across country by the stars. Although he had no fear of being lost with the dark ridge of the San Luis Hills on the left to guide him, it added to his sense of angry futility not to know precisely where he was on his own range. At last his slow progress was stopped by the wide and deep arroyo of Hard Creek, risky if not impassable at this point in the dark. Instinct told him that he had struck the creek above the ranch; he turned west, therefore, following the arroyo downstream until the lights of the house came into view, seeming faint and distant as if miles away. Some minutes later, the tired gelding found the trail at last and without guidance picked its way down the steep arroyo wall, across the brushy flat and the small summer trickle of water, and up the precipitous path on the far side. Ten minutes more of riding, on familiar ground now, brought them into the yard.

Attracted by the sound of an approaching horse, Jim McCloud had come down the path from the house and a couple of the hands had emerged from the bunkhouse. Parrish thought they all looked a little surprised to see him; he remembered that he had announced his intention of spending the night in town. He climbed stiffly from the saddle and started to say something to explain his change in plan, and thought better of it. Passing the reins to the nearest rider, he turned on his heel and walked quickly up the path and into the house. A lamp burned by the desk, where McCloud had apparently been working over the ranch accounts. After a moment, Parrish heard the older man enter the room behind him. He did not look around and McCloud did not speak for a while, and then only to ask, "Had dinner, Captain?" When Parrish shook his head, the foreman said, "I'll have Tony rustle you up something."

The kitchen door opened and the cook's voice said, "Tony is already rustling up. Here is coffee while you wait."

When the cook had left the room, Parrish looked at Jim McCloud. "They offered me four thousand," he said softly. "I have twenty-four hours to think it over."

The foreman said, "It don't look like Lew Wilkison's going to bankrupt himself overbidding on the place, for a fact."

Parrish made an abrupt gesture with his hand. "The hell of it is, Jim, it's enough. With what we made last year, thanks to your management, it'll do. Oh, I'll lose a little money, but I'll be able to pay back most of what I borrowed to come out here; and after all, I did come out for my health, and I've got that. And Caroline wants to go East, and I promised her. . . . I promised her I'd accept any fair offer." He grimaced, and pushed his hand across his mouth as if to rub the expression away. "Do you consider four thousand dollars a fair offer for Rafter H, Jim?"

The older man said uncomfortably, "What do you want me to say, Captain?"

"I want you to tell me the truth," Parrish said quietly. "I want you to tell me that it's a raw steal. The question is, Jim, am I going to stand for it?" A sudden harshness came into his voice. "Do you know the answer to that, Jim?"

"Captain, I—"

Parrish said roughly, "Well, the answer is yes, Jim! I'm going to stand for it. Oh, I'll make it look good. I'll go back tomorrow and dicker with them. I'll tell them they can have it for six, and they'll split the difference with me and settle for five; the girl said so. I didn't come out here

66

to fight a war, and they know it, but God damn it, they'd better not laugh where I can hear them or I'll take that fancy gun away from that two-bit hardcase and shove it down his throat butt-first! I don't care how big he is. I gave orders to bigger men than that, and saw that they were obeyed. I know all about big men who think they are something to be afraid of; I've been coming up against size all my life. If there's anything I love it's big, tough men who think they've got the world by the tail; there's always some way to trip up a man who's too big for his hat, and I'm just the boy who can find it!" He raised his fist to slam it down against the table, but realized that this was a silly and melodramatic thing to do and checked the impulse. His anger evaporated as quickly as it had built up; he laughed at himself and at his foreman's expression. "Forget it, Jim. I just had to let off a little steam. It goes against the grain to let myself be booted out of this place with a nickel in my pocket, as if I were a fat, frightened old man like Jack Mahoney. But that's pride, Jim, and I saw too many proud men get themselves and a lot of other people killed in the war, proving nothing whatsoever. . . . What's the matter now?"

"Why, nothing," the older man said. "Nothing at all, Captain. It was just—well, for a moment there you had me scared. I thought you was going to turn out human after all, with a temper and everything."

He turned toward the door. Parrish stopped him. "Jim."

McCloud looked back over his shoulder. "What is it, Captain?"

"Temper is something only the very strong or the very rich can afford, Jim. That's something my father taught me early."

"Your dad did a good job of teaching," the older man said. "Good night, Captain."

"Good night, Jim."

After the door had closed, Parrish looked at it for a moment grimly, shrugged his shoulders, and picked up the mug of coffee from the table. Drinking the hot liquid, he found himself wishing that he had, after all, ridden to town; Caroline would have sympathized with his feelings and appreciated the wisdom of his decision. It frightened him a little to realize that he did not want her sympathy or appreciation. He had, he discovered, no respect for her judgment and very little faith in her motives. It shocked him deeply to understand that the one thing he wanted from Caroline Vail right now was something he could have had from any complaisant woman; it revealed an emptiness to their relationship that was a little terrifying.

He swung about and strode into the kitchen, to find his dinner ready. "Dinner all hours of the night is not good," the cook said reproachfully. "Next time you let me know, I make it better, *si?*"

"*Si*, Antonio," Parrish said, sitting down to eat.

"This Wilkison he make trouble for you, Señor?"

Parrish said, "Well, he's trying, you've got to hand him that, Antonio. He's trying hard."

He looked up as Joe DeRosa came into the kitchen, removing his hat. "Mr. Parrish, Jim wants me to tell you we just heard a bunch of riders hightailing it down the main road; must have come either out of the Hills or from over Silas Purdue's way. Jim wants to know if you think we should do anything about it."

"Do?" Parrish asked. "Such as?"

"Well," the rider said, "Jim seemed to think maybe old Silas had run into trouble of some kind."

Parrish said, "Last time Mr. Purdue was here, he didn't sound as if he was interested in our help."

DeRosa nodded, as if hearing a theory confirmed. "Jim figured you'd think that way. I'll tell him."

Parrish pushed his plate aside and got to his feet, reaching for his hat. "Keep it warm for me, Antonio. I'll be back." He walked grimly past DeRosa, who made way for him with a show of respect that lacked sincerity. McCloud was waiting in the yard. "All right, Jim," Parrish said. "What is it now? How many riders?"

"Eight or ten, by the sound."

"Heading toward town?"

"Or toward Anchor. In the dark, going around by the road would be almost as quick and a lot easier than cutting across country."

"But you don't know," Parrish said. "And Mr. Purdue has warned us to stay off Box Seven. What you heard could have been just a bunch of Hills folk. It's Saturday night, remember."

"A little late for that, Captain. They won't reach town before midnight, if that's where they're going." McCloud spat into the dust at his feet. "First it was Jack Mahoney, then the sheriff, then us. I figure they're not going to neglect Box Seven forever; and they're not going to bother making Silas any offers, since they know he won't sell."

Parrish said, "Ah, hell, Jim, you're bound to get me into this, one way or another, aren't you?" He drew a long, impatient breath. "All right, saddle me up something that won't fall over its feet in the dark while I finish my dinner. We'll go take a look. I owe the Purdues that much in spite of what the old man—"

He broke off, and they all heard it: the shuffle and scrape of a tired horse approaching at a walk from the direction of the Hills. A moment later it appeared around the corner of the bunkhouse, a dark pony moving with a curious, exaggerated care, so as not to dislodge the bowed figure clinging to the saddlehorn. The pony came to a halt in the center of the yard. Parrish and McCloud reached it in time to catch the rider as he started to spill loosely to the ground.

"It's Bud," McCloud said.

Parrish said, "Let's get him up to the house."

"Bunkhouse is closer, Captain." The foreman's voice had a cold, withdrawn sound. "A couple of you boys give me a hand here!" he snapped. "Easy now, the lad's been shot; slip a blanket under him and grab the corners. . . ."

Parrish found himself shouldered aside. He watched the unconscious form of Bud Hinkleman being carried gently into the bunkhouse. After a moment, he glanced down at his hands, which had blood on them. He wiped them clean. The tired horse was still standing where it had halted, head down. Parrish looked toward the bunkhouse door. Instinct told him that he was not wanted inside; these men looked out for their own, and he was not one of them. He turned away and busied himself taking care of the pony.

69

Presently McCloud appeared in the doorway with Joe DeRosa. "Ride like hell, Joe," the foreman said. "Tell Doc Kinsman it looks bad. . . . Captain, he wants you."

Parrish looked up, slapped the pony on the rump, and walked quickly over to where the older man was waiting. They looked at each other for a moment. Parrish thought, *They gave me twenty-four hours; how could I know?* But he did not say this aloud; it was not a time for self-justification. He brushed past McCloud and walked slowly down the long, cluttered room to the bunk at which the other men were standing. They made way for him. The sight of Bud Hinkleman's face in the yellow lamplight was a dual shock to Parrish; outside it had not been apparent that the boy had taken a bad beating, nor had it been obvious that he was dying. Parrish, who had seen men die before, knew instantly that DeRosa was riding on a fruitless errand. He tried to keep the knowledge out of his face and voice.

"How's it coming, Bud?" he asked.

The boy opened his eyes. "My fault," he whispered. "Slept too heavy. All around the cabin before I could get my boots and gun . . . got the drop on me . . . didn't expect . . . didn't expect . . ."

Parrish said, "It's all right. Nothing you could have helped, Bud. Don't worry about it."

"They said—" Bud Hinkleman licked his lips weakly, "—said to tell you it was to . . . to help you make up your mind."

"Who said that?"

"Fellow was running things, young fellow, fancy clothes, two guns, they called him Kid, he beat me up while two of them held me. Then . . . then they started to fire the cabin. I . . . I kicked this Kid fellow—" a faint smile came to Bud Hinkleman's lips, "—kicked like hell where it hurt him and tried to get my gun, it was on the ground, but they caught me . . . and the Kid fellow straightened up and I saw what he was going to do and he shot me. While they was holding me." He licked his lips again. "The others, they didn't like that much. Heard them arguing and carrying on. Cabin burning. Couple of them . . .

saddled my pony and lifted me on . . . don't remember
. . . turned me loose near the ranch. . . . Didn't think I
was going to . . . make it. . . ."

Parrish said gently, "Well, you made it all right, Bud."
Then he saw that the boy was dead.

11

■ Acting Sheriff Magruder was a big man running to
fat that tended to bulge out over the buckle of his belt.
The most prominent feature of his face was a great, straggling black mustache. His eyes had a sunken, permanently
squinting look, so that no matter what the time of the
day or the state of the weather this man would always
seem to be suffering a little from sunlight too bright to
bear. He walked across the uneven floor of Gosnell's undertaking establishment with the deliberate gait of the
overweight and stood for a moment before the body on
the table, removing his hat as an afterthought.

Turning, he said, "You'll be Parrish, out to Rafter H, I
take it. That's one of your men?"

"That's right, Sheriff."

"Kind of young, ain't he? Name's Hinkleman, you say?
There's a nester family named Hinkleman down near
South Meadows, as I recall. Since when have cattlemen
been hiring nester brats to do their riding for them?"

Jim McCloud started to speak angrily, but Parrish
waved him into silence. "Isn't that a little beside the point,
Sheriff? he asked. "Frankly, I didn't know where the boy
came from, and I doubt that my foreman did either, when
he hired him. But he worked hard and was willing to

71

learn. Now he's dead. We expect the law to take care of his murderer."

"Um," the sheriff said. "Well, Mr. Parrish, we've got what you might call a peculiar situation here. You see, after listening to the feller you sent across the street to fetch me. I went on up to Pat Morgan's place, which is why I'm a little late getting here. Happens I'd seen this Kid feller in there a little earlier in the evening. Well, I tell you, Mr. Parrish, now, I don't rightly know what to do." He scratched his head, as if to emphasize his perplexity.

Parrish asked, "What seems to be the difficulty?"

Magruder said, "Well, here's you and half a dozen of your hands telling me this Pecos feller's guilty of murder —leastways I suppose you've all got the same story. But the trouble is, there's twice as many Anchor hands over there will take their oath the boy never stepped out of Morgan's since four this afternoon; and Pat Morgan and his house-men will back up that statement. So it looks to me, Mr. Parrish, like this dead boy must have made a mistake about who shot him, or you and your men misheard what he was trying to tell you."

"I see," Parrish said softly. He was aware of his crew watching him, waiting to see what he would do about this; and he felt his hands trying to close into tight fists at his sides, but he did not let them. "In other words, Sheriff, you don't feel justified in making an arrest?"

Magruder made a theatrically helpless gesture. "Now, Mr. Parrish, with over a dozen people willing to take their oath this feller was in town when the murder was committed, how can I arrest him just on the strength of what somebody tells me a dying man's supposed to have said? It isn't even as if I had a written deathbed statement to go on!"

Parrish said, "I could swear out a warrant."

"I reckon you could do that," the sheriff agreed pleasantly. "Judge French will fix one up for you, if you really want it. You know where he lives, up on the hill?" He frowned at Parrish's expression, as if hurt. "Oh, I'd serve it, all right," he said. "As an officer of the law, I'd be bound to, wouldn't I? I'd put the boy in jail and see that he got to trial the way the law provides. But just between you and me, Mr. Parrish, I've got a hunch he'd be acquitted. A man can't be two places at once. He can't be committing murder and arson out in the San Loos while he's having a friendly game of poker in Logasa. I reckon a jury wouldn't take long to turn him loose, after they'd heard the testimony. After all, Mr. Parrish, nothing personal intended, but out here we don't take kindly to have strangers come among us and get rich off our land and try to use our law to settle their private grudges. I'd think it over real careful like before I started making out warrants for people's arrest."

Parrish kept his expression neutral. "All right, Sheriff," he said without emphasis. "All right. Thank you for the advice."

Magruder wheeled his heavy body toward the door, then swung back to squint at Parrish suspiciously. "Just one more thing, Mr. Parrish. There'll be no lynchings in my jurisdiction, do you understand? Get your men out of town or see that they behave peacefully or I'll throw the lot of them in jail."

They watched him turn and walk out through the open door. The silence endured until they could no longer hear the sound of the heavy, receding footsteps. Then there, was a simultaneous scuffing of booted feet in the room. Parrish took three steps forward and swung about, blocking the door. "Where the hell," he demanded, "do you think you're going?"

The habit of command was something that stayed with a man, and his voice checked them. He faced them from the doorway, seeing the wildness that burned at them like fire; even McCloud's patience was stretched thin, and his pale gray eyes looked flat and cruel. The savagery in the faces confronting him helped Parrish to control his own anger. Someone had to use some common sense here, and the job was clearly his, since these men were in his employ.

Yet instinct told him that he had already failed. They had listened to him once. Wanting to ride against Anchor immediately, they had let him persuade them to bring the

73

body into town first and report the matter to the law. It had been a gamble, and he had lost it; the law had not only refused to act, it had, ironically, let them know that the man they wanted was right here, close at hand. He frowned at the thought, as it occurred to him that the sheriff had talked very stupidly for a man who wanted to keep the peace, and he had not seemed like a stupid man.

Joe DeRosa stepped forward. "Get out of the way, Mr. Parrish. We're through listening to you!"

McCloud put a hand on the dark-haired rider's arm, restraining him. He spoke softly: "Captain, coming from the East, you wouldn't understand about the way we look at these things out here. If you'll kindly step aside—"

Parrish studied them for a moment longer. They were all here and they were all armed tonight, even the cook, who carried a muzzle-loading rifle with a long, octagonal barrel. Parrish studied each man in turn as the silence grew heavier; he found that an old habit, well learned, that he had thought forgotten, made him tonight regard each one, not as a man but as an effective fighting unit. DeRosa's equipment was in good shape, he saw, but the man had a rashness about him that would get him into trouble. Harry Germack's gun and belt looked well cared for, like all of this rider's possessions; Jackson's leather was scuffed and worn, and there was no bluing left on the visible metal parts of his pistol, but the weapon was not rusty. Wash Breed, the oldest member of the crew, wore his gun simply thrust into the waistband of his trousers. McCloud carried a carbine as well as a holstered revolver.

They were good men; yet for a moment, impatient with them, he saw them as a scratch, undisciplined lot who would let anger and grief cloud their thinking to the point where anyone with an elementary sense of strategy could trap them and wipe them out. Yet it was clear that nothing he could say would deter them. He made a gesture of surrender and moved to one side. "I'll have nothing to do with it," he said loudly. "You heard what the sheriff said. You can't take the law into your own hands, men—"

DeRosa spat on the floor. "You just watch us, Mr. Parrish!"

Parrish laughed in a grim way. "Watch you get killed, you mean."

It stopped them at the door. DeRosa said impatiently, "Ah, don't listen to him!"

McCloud hesitated, and turned. "What's on your mind, Captain?"

"Why, nothing," Parrish said. "I'm washing my hands of it; and your lives are your own. I'll interfere with no man who's bent on committing suicide."

DeRosa said harshly, "Mr. Parrish, we're going over to Morgan's and take that feller out. Don't try to stop us with trick words!"

Parrish shrugged. "Go ahead," he said. "Of course, you know there'll be more than a dozen men waiting for you inside, and that the sheriff will throw a screen of deputies across the street behind you the minute you move out into the open. He made all that quite plain; obviously he came here for nothing but to goad us into taking action. Anchor would naturally prefer to wipe us out in a legal manner."

McCloud frowned, thinking this over, and even DeRosa was silent. "What would you suggest, Captain?" the foreman asked at last.

Parrish said, "Why, don't ask me, Jim. I'll have no part in it. . . . Of course, if I was doing it, I suppose I'd ride out of town peacefully to let them think I was giving up the idea. Then I'd wait for them at some suitable point on the road to Anchor. That way I'd have just the Anchor bunch to deal with, instead of having to take on Morgan and his house-men and all the law in the county as well." He cleared his throat abruptly. "Of course, that's just a manner of speaking. I've no intention of sharing in such high-handed and illegal proceedings; and I want to make it clear that those who persist in this action are no longer working for Rafter H." He put his hat on his head, with an air of finality. "Well, I'm going up to the Vails' now to spend the night, but I'll head back to the ranch in the morning. If you change your minds, I'll be glad to see you there; if not, I'll have your pay ready for you. Good night."

He turned away from them, went back to the table upon

which the dead boy lay, and paused there for a moment; then he swung back and walked out of the place. They moved aside to let him through the door. Outside, the moon was high behind him. It was so late at night that even Front Street was growing quiet; when a woman in Hannessey's place let out a shrill and drunken laugh, it seemed to echo through the town. A man came out of Morgan's far up the street. He mounted a horse and came riding toward Parrish, who watched him approach and go past. Neither the man nor the brand on his horse was familiar.

Behind him he could hear the voices of his own men raised in agrument. DeRosa would be for action, McCloud for caution; and McCloud would probably swing them, since they were used to taking his orders. Parrish climbed wearily aboard the small, white-footed mare he had ridden to town; it had been a long day of riding, searching the limits of his new-found strength. He let the mare move up the street at a walk, swung left into Hill Street, and stopped there, waiting in the shadows. Presently he saw McCloud come striding out of the undertaking parlor, followed by the rest of the crew. The cook climbed to the seat of the buckboard and turned the vehicle around while the others mounted. Parrish watched them all ride away from him, the buckboard jolting in the ruts of the street.

When they had gone out of sight, he allowed himself a long breath of relief. Only then did he look at the object he had removed from the table by Bud Hinkleman's body and slipped under his coat. The boy's gun gleamed dully in the pale light. Parrish removed it from the holster. It was empty; some Anchor rider had apparently removed the cartridges and returned the weapon to its owner after the shooting, perhaps as a kind of apology. There were extra cartridges in the belt. Parrish loaded the gun fully and buckled the belt about him. He felt some regret for what he was about to do, but not as much as he had expected. A man could waste his life regretting the inevitable.

12

■ Riding up to the hitching rack in front of Morgan's saloon, Parrish felt no fear, nor any other emotion. It was always that way, he remembered; the fear came later, or earlier. When you were moving into action there was no time for it. The whole thing was clear in his mind now. He dismounted and gave the reins a turn about the worn rail and looked about him uneasily as a frightened man might. He rubbed his hands along his thighs as if to dry them, in a furtive manner. A man stood by the swinging doors, idly watching him. Another leaned against the corner of the building, smoking a cigarette. Both were armed. From inside came the sound of a piano, of a man's voice, and of a woman's laughter.

Parrish thought, *He will be at least a little drunk, and he will be thinking himself a big and dangerous man who has killed two here, perhaps more elsewhere. Because I am a dude he will have no respect for me at all. These are the things I have to work with.* There was in him no mercy at all; only a flicker of returning anger, and a grim bitterness at the necessity for this. *They couldn't wait,* he thought; *they would have had it at their own price tomorrow, but they couldn't even wait out their own time limit!* He ducked beneath the rail and stepped up to the boardwalk in front of the place. The man by the door, a lean, sandy-haired individual, watched him and said nothing.

Parrish moved forward, past this man, pushed the doors open, and stepped inside. The man turned with him and followed him in, and Parrish felt something touch his back gently, and knew what this was. "Right there's far enough,

77

Mr. Parrish," the man behind him said, and he stopped.

Saturday nights were usually busy ones for Morgan's, but this was the tail end of the evening and there were not more than twenty customers in the long room, scattered about the various tables; half a dozen women kept them company. The men had a dull and sodden look; the women's faces looked worn and their bright dresses tarnished. As Parrish stood there, the room gradually became silent, and the women, one after another, slipped out of sight in a casual way, as if the situation was one they recognized from past experience. The piano stopped playing. Then one of the batwing doors that led to a side alley crashed open, and a man stumbled in, breathless.

"They rode out of town, Pecos," he panted. "They'll be laying for us on the road; old Gosnell, the undertaker, heard them talking. That dude owner of theirs backed out of the deal and went to see his girl; last I saw of him he was heading up Hill Street—"

He recognized Parrish by the other door and fell abruptly silent. Somebody snickered. At the bar, which ran along the right hand wall of the big room, the Pecos Kid turned, shoving his black hat back from his forehead. His face and figure looked very young—the wide, ornate double gun-belt with its heavy, matched revolvers seemed an unfair burden for his narrow body—but there was an old evil in his eyes and cruelty in the set of his mouth. This was a boy to whom killing had become a pleasure. Parrish had seen them in the war and knew the signs.

The kid made a show of being slow to become aware of his presence. Parrish did not speak. The boy looked him up and down for a space of time.

"Looking for somebody, Buster?" he asked at last, softly.

"Why, I guess so," Parrish said uncertainly. "I guess I'm looking for a fellow who calls himself the Pecos Kid. The sheriff mentioned he was in here."

"You're looking at him," the boy at the bar said. A glint of feeling in his eyes indicated that he did not like not being recognized. The men on either side of him had moved away now, leaving him alone. "What do you want with the Pecos Kid, Buster?"

"Well," Parrish said, and licked his lips. "Well, I don't really know how to say this." He started forward, and checked himself. "You see, I own a ranch out in the Basin —my name's Parrish incidentally—and one of my men was killed this evening. . . . Is it all right if I move?"

The Kid frowned. "What the hell are you talking about?"

"Well, this gentleman behind me—he seems to have a gun against my back. At least I presume it's a gun. I—" Parrish removed his hat and drew a sleeve across his forehead. "I think I would like a drink, if you don't mind," he said weakly.

He heard them laughing at him now. It was a measure of success; aside from that it had no other meaning. More men had died from fear of being laughed at than from any other cause, and he could recall his father telling him that one aspect of genius was knowing when to act like a fool. At the Kid's nod, the gun in his back was withdrawn, and he walked forward, men making way for him amusedly. He could feel the beating of his heart shaking him now, and was annoyed with himself for not being able to control it. *Closer,* he thought as the distance shortened, *closer, much closer, you can't be too close for this.* When he was face to face with the Kid, he stopped. They had the bar to themselves now. The Kid pushed something toward him.

"There's your drink, Buster. Toss it down like a little man."

Parrish took the small, heavy glass and managed to let half the liquor spill out of it as he raised it; then he swallowed and coughed. There was more laughter in the room, but it was a distant roaring sound, without meaning. He looked at the Kid and saw the thing in sharp detail; the boy was leaning against the bar lazily, putting his left gun out of action, which simplified matters considerably.

"Have another," the Kid said.

"No," Parrish said, and cleared his throat. "One is my limit. Doctor's orders."

"Buster, your doctor should see you now."

There was a sneering note to the boy's voice, and his eyes, mean and bloodshot, lightened with satisfaction as men laughed anew at his sally. He said, "So one of your men was killed this evening. You wouldn't be hinting I did it, would you, Buster?"

The way the words were spoken, and the snickers they provoked from some of the men would have satisfied Parrish, if he had had any doubts at all, that he had come to the right place. He made an awkward gesture.

"Well, he *said* you did it."

"You shouldn't believe everything you hear, Buster."

"Why, I don't," Parrish said. "I certainly don't, Mr. Pecos. That's why I came here to talk to you. The men seemed to think we ought to—to punish you ourselves, since the sheriff wouldn't take any action, but I certainly wouldn't countenance anything of the kind. I mean, you can't take the law into your own hands, can you? But the men seemed quite determined, and I'm very much afraid they're going to get themselves into trouble, so I thought if I could talk to you and persuade you to give yourself up and stand trial—"

It went like clockwork. The Kid stared at him for a moment unbelievingly. Then he threw back his head in a joyous whoop of laughter that was echoed throughout the room, and in that moment Parrish, left-handed, reached up and pulled the black hat hard down over the other's eyes, He felt no scruples at all, remembering an old man dead in the street and a boy dying in the bunkhouse at Rafter H. He kept the same hand moving, slashing down between their bodies, sweeping aside the long barrel of the gun that seemed to leap into the Kid's hand even before the other had fought free of the hat that was blinding him. The heavy revolver discharged, the flash from the cylinder scorching Parrish's wrist as he grasped for the weapon desperately; then his own gun was clear and he felt the smash of the recoil as it fired, the muzzle almost touching the body of the youth in front of him. He let the weapon's throw raise it a little for each subsequent shot.

The world seemed full of the crash of firearms and the garlic smell of black powder. Some marksman's instinct made him keep count of the shots from his own weapon and stop at five, reserving the last bullet. Suddenly there was silence. He stepped back. In his left hand, he discovered, he was holding an ivory-handled revolver by the barrel as one might hold a bottle by the neck. Then the figure in front of him started to fall.

13

■ Riding away, Parrish heard the frozen silence of the saloon break into tumult behind him, now that the threat of his gun was withdrawn. There were men on Front Street now—and women also—attracted toward Morgan's by the sound of shooting. They jumped aside to let him pass. Parrish thought he heard the sheriff's voice behind him, calling to him to stop; but he paid no attention to this, and no one shot at him. As he pulled the mare down to a canter beyond the edge of town, a group of riders came at him around a curve in the road. He reined in, seeking a new direction for flight, but a moment later he had recognized the approaching horsemen as his own crew.

They stopped around him. McCloud said, "Everything all right, Captain? We heard shooting in town."

Parrish said, "Everything is fine, Jim."

The old foreman studied him in the moonlight, sensing a puzzle here; then his glance fell to the wide, carved double gun-belt that was slung from his employer's saddle horn. He studied the ivory-handled guns for a moment, urged his horse forward a pace, and ran his finger along the belt. Something came off the leather, and he examined this and tested the consistency of it thoughtfully between thumb and forefinger, finally wiping it off on his trousers. He looked at Parrish again, with an odd, startled expression in his eyes.

"You damn young fool," he said softly.

Parrish said, "Let's go. They'll be along any minute. Where did you leave Tony and the buckboard?"

McCloud did not move at once. There was anger in his voice when he spoke again. "You sent us away and walked into that place alone? All that fancy talk you gave us was nothing but foolbait to get us out of town? Son, I could get downright provoked—"

Parrish said impatiently, "One man could do it. Six couldn't. You wanted a man dead. Well, he's dead. What the hell are you complaining about, Jim?" After a moment he added, in a different tone, "Bud was working for me, not you, Jim. I paid his wages and I was responsible for him. Now let's get moving before we have a fight on our hands."

"Ah, hell—"

McCloud checked himself and kicked his horse around. After a moment, the rest of the crew followed suit, riding behind Parrish and the foreman in silence. Presently there was an audible chuckle, and DeRosa's voice said, "Well, I'll be damned! I sure would have liked to see the Kid's face. Here he was thinking himself a real tough hombre, and a little dude from the East walks in and—"

Parrish said in a harsh voice, "I saw his face, DeRosa. I didn't find it amusing."

There was no more conversation. Presently they turned up a wagon track to fetch the cook, waiting in a sheltered place with the buckboard. While they were about this, they heard the Anchor crew go by on the main road. The dust of their passing was still in the air when Parrish and his companions swung into the road again, heading in the same direction, but at a pace governed by the cook's team. Riding beside McCloud, Parrish could hear the men beginning to talk in low tones behind him, and he did not doubt that he was the subject of their conversation. The thought gave him no pleasure at all.

There was a terrible burden upon him at this moment.

82

He knew that if his relationship with Caroline Vail had been that which should have existed between a man and a woman about to be married, he would have turned back and gone to her now, because he needed her help. But he knew there would be no help for him there, only recriminations. His reaction to having killed a man would not concern her, only the fact that by doing so he had hopelessly involved himself in the affairs of this place that she wanted so desperately to leave.

She would see, as he did, that what had happened tonight was only a beginning of something that could grow and spread till it engulfed the whole Basin, and that he was a part of it now, whether he wanted to be or not. *Now?* he thought. *Why, I have been a part of it for three years!* You could not buy land and live on it, hire men and live and work with them; you could not find your health in a country, and even something that had, at least for a time, resembled love, without giving the country something of yourself in return.

He made the startling discovery that to him the East had, without his realizing it, become a shadowy place peopled only by remembered names, not actual persons; he knew suddenly that he had no desire at all to go back and pick up the routine of the life he had been leading before his illness had become critical. The thought of spending the rest of his life in an office was repellent; the thought of leaving Rafter H in other hands, no matter whose, was unbearable. He had not yet started to learn all the things he needed to know; he had not begun a fraction of the projects he wanted to carry out. . . .

He checked his horse where the road branched off to the left, toward Anchor, and sat for a moment in thought, aware of the crew watching him curiously. Presently he turned to McCloud.

"Take the boys on home, Jim," he said.

The old foreman asked irritably, "Captain, what kind of a rabbit-brained idea have you got in your head now?"

"I'm going to Anchor," Parrish said. "Maybe some strong talk can put a stop to this killing before it goes any further."

"You won't do much talking with a bullet through you. Are you crazy, son? What do you think will happen to you, showing up there tonight?"

Parrish said, "Nothing will happen to me. The Pecos Kid wasn't the kind who'd have friends after he's dead. I'll be all right, if you don't get a wild notion of trailing after me and protecting me. That'll certainly get me killed, when they spot you. Just ride along home, Jim." He waited and nothing happened. He made his voice crisp in a remembered fashion. "That's an order, McCloud!"

The older man cleared his throat and spat, unimpressed.

"Yes, sir, Captain Parrish, sir," he said dryly. "Come on, boys."

It was a long ten miles to Anchor from the fork in the road, and weariness pressed down on Parrish as the little mare carried him endlessly onward through the fading moonlight. He found himself dozing in the saddle; there was something terribly familiar about this, and it seemed strange to be riding alone. He found himself remembering the smell and taste and sound of a cavalry movement in the dark. . . .

He roused abruptly and saw the lights of Anchor ahead of him. A rider had closed in on him from either side; he looked into the muzzle of a rifle in the hands of a man he did not know. The second rider, however, was no stranger; it was the lean and sandy-haired man who had put a gun into his back as he walked into Morgan's.

The first man said, "I'll be damned if it isn't the dude himself! What the hell do you think you're doing here, Red?"

"I want to talk to Hansen and Mr. Wilkison," Parrish said.

"Reckon they'll be glad to oblige you," the spokesman said dryly. "Take him up to the house, Phil. I'll stick around here. Keep your eyes open; the little bastard's trickier than he looks, as the Kid found out tonight."

He laughed, showing no signs of grief, and turned his horse off the road, where horse and rider seemed to blend instantly with the darkness of the hollow, into which the low moon could no longer reach. The man called Phil had brought his carbine from the scabbard. He signed to Parrish to move on, and Parrish kicked the mare into motion again, with Phil riding alongside. The sandy-haired man's voice came presently: "So the young feller died. I was afraid he was shot bad."

Parrish glanced at him, a little surprised. "Bud Hinkleman?"

"Was that his name? I didn't know."

Parrish asked, "Was it you who put him on his horse and brought him by the ranch?"

"Me and a couple of others who don't like to see men shot in the back, or when their arms are held." After a while, the man said, "Name's Phil Bennett. You might keep it in mind, Mr. Parrish."

"Why should I do that?"

"I ride for Mr. Wilkison, not for Cole Hansen or any of his hired gun-boys."

"Is there a difference?"

"Not now, but there might be some day." Phil Bennett hesitated, and went on: "No matter what they tell you about Anchor, Mr. Parrish, this used to be a good place for a man to work, some years back. But there's not many of the old crew left around here now, and the old man's got some bee in his bonnet that Hansen and Miss Martha put there. Just the same, you might keep in mind that Mr. Wilkison's one man and Cole Hansen's another; and that the old man's not quite as old or as dumb as some people seem to think." Bennett gave Parrish a quick glance, and said in a sharper tone, "Ah, hell, I talk too damn much. It'll be the death of me yet. If you can bear to kick that nag once more, maybe we'll get up to the house before sunrise."

They trotted up the long drive, between the trees, to the big veranda. A rather tall, quite slender figure came forward to meet them, and Parrish recognized Judith Wilkison, in a plain blue robe of some rough and mannish material, faded from long wear. Her light-brown hair was loose about her shoulders, making her seem more feminine than he remembered her. She looked at him for a moment, clearly startled at seeing him here.

85

"This is a strange place for you to come tonight, cowboy," she said, and glanced at Bennett, who had dismounted and was waiting for Parrish to do the same. Judith held out her hand. "Give me the rifle, Phil; I'll watch him. You get Dad and Cole; they're in the study."

"All right, Miss Judy."

When he had gone into the house, Judith turned back to Parrish, the rifle thrown casually over her arm. "Light down," she said.

"I'm comfortable," Parrish said.

She moved her shoulders briefly. "I suppose I owe you an apology," she said after a moment.

"How so?"

."I accused you of being a clever and careful man. It would seem that you have proved me wrong."

A perverse honesty made Parrish answer, "There was no great risk, Miss Wilkison. The boy was drunk and over-confident, and his companions expected no trouble from a tenderfoot. They were too surprised to take action. I counted on that."

A faint smile touched her lips. "You make it sound as if you shot him down in cold blood."

Parrish said, "I pulled his hat over his eyes and put five bullets through his body. I am not a gentleman where guns are concerned, Miss Wilkison. Dueling has always seemed to me a remarkably stupid business."

"And coming here?" the girl murmured, seeming oddly amused. "You don't consider that risky?"

Parrish said, "It's a gamble. I'm counting on your father's pride to keep me alive until I'm off the premises. I doubt that he'd countenance the open shooting of a man who had come here on a mission of peace."

"Oh," she said dryly, "is that what you are here for, peace?"

"It's something for which I have been searching a long time," Parrish said. "It seems to be a difficult thing to find."

"It's pretty damn scarce around here, Mr. Parrish," Judith Wilkison said. "You've picked a poor lode to mine. But I wish you luck."

She turned to watch her father's wheelchair propelled through the front door by the big hands of Cole Hansen, whose figure loomed black and tall against the light, dwarfing the seated figure of the crippled man. Phil Bennett, following them out, retrieved his rifle from the girl and leaned against one of the white pillars in a negligent manner, as Mr. Wilkison, with an impatient gesture, had himself halted at the edge of the veranda. He wore a dressing-gown and his white hair was rumpled as if he had been in bed. His blue eyes stared fiercely up at Parrish, and for a moment these two faced each other thus, locked in a silent battle in which there could be no victory. Abruptly Parrish reached down, disengaged the ornate gun-belt from his saddle horn, and threw it clattering to the boards of the porch.

"There's your hired murderer, Mr. Wilkison," he said softly. "The one you claimed you had booted off your ranch with a sore tail."

A flush deepened the redness of Lew Wilkison's face to an extent visible even in the poor light. Parrish saw that the old man seemed uncomfortable, and that he glanced resentfully toward Cole Hansen, as if blaming his son-in-law for putting him in an intolerable position. He cleared his throat.

"All right, son," he said in a surprisingly gentle voice. "Now you've got the play-acting off your chest, maybe you can tell me what you've got to say that's worth staying up at this hour to listen to."

Parrish said, "Early this afternoon you made me an offer for my ranch and gave me twenty-four hours to think it over. I'm bringing you the answer: Rafter H is not for sale." He shifted in the saddle so that he could see the men who had drifted up to witness this, and pitched his voice so that they could all hear him. "I've decided to stay here, Mr. Wilkison," he said. "You haven't got enough money to buy me out, or enough men to drive me out. I don't mean that as a challenge; I'm simply stating a fact. I can hold Rafter H against anything you can throw against me. Don't deceive yourself otherwise, Mr. Wilkison; or you either, Hansen."

The younger man stirred, and Parrish looked at him for a moment, but Hansen did not speak, and Parrish looked back to Lew Wilkison. He said, "Therefore, we're going to be neighbors for a long time, Mr. Wilkison. It's up to you whether we live together peaceably, or throw the whole Basin into open conflict." He drew a long breath. "This is what I came here to say, Mr. Wilkison. Please don't make the mistake of underestimating me again, as your tame killer did tonight. I know I have a way of riding that seems funny to you, and I'm not a big man, and I don't know much about cattle; but don't let that fool you into thinking that you can hit me without being hit back. You can't. There's nothing you can do on my range that I can't do on yours, and you have more to lose than I have. Don't make me fight; I assure you that you won't like my way of fighting. Stay on your own range. We can get along, if you'll only let us."

14

■ The following morning had an odd and unreal quality to John Parrish. The events of the night seemed remote and indistinct, as if they had happened to another person; he could not recall the details of the long ride home. He was startled to discover the soreness of his left wrist, scorched and pitted blackly by the discharge of the Pecos Kid's gun. At breakfast he was aware of the men watching him curiously; he knew that he had stepped out of the character they had made for him over the past few years, and they did not quite know what to expect of him now.

Toward noon, George Menefee drove up to the ranch

in a rented buggy. Parrish, recognizing his voice greeting McCloud in the yard, went out onto the porch to meet the lawyer and they shook hands politely.

"Good morning, John," Menefee said. "Or is it 'Lightning Red' Parrish these days? In town they are saying you took on the whole Anchor crew last night, single-handed."

"That report is a little exaggerated," Parrish said. "Come in and have some coffee."

"I thank you," Menefee said. "I accept the invitation, but you had better go down there." He jerked his head toward the buggy in the yard. "Caroline is with me. She insisted on coming. She wants to see you."

Parrish felt an involuntary shudder go down his spine. "All right," he said.

"You'd better approach cautiously," Menefee said cheerfully. "She's not pleased with you. I'll wait up here."

The sun was bright and hot as Parrish moved down the steep path from the house. Although the men had all been instructed to stay close to the ranch today, none of them was in sight at the moment. The buggy stood alone by the gate. Caroline looked around quickly as he stopped beside her.

"Oh, there you are!" she said, swinging to face him.

He studied her for a moment in silence. She was wearing a neat blue suit with a matching bonnet; her gloves were white, and there was white at her throat. He had seldom seen her dressed in this fashionable manner, at least of late, and he knew a stab of sympathy for her as he noted that the heat of the day and the dust of the long drive had noticeably impaired the perfection of the picture she had doubtless intended for him to see—a fact of which she was clearly aware, and which did not improve her disposition toward him.

"Well?" she said sharply; and when he did not speak: "It seems to me I'm entitled to an explanation, honey! It's the first time I've found myself engaged to a murderer, and I declare I don't quite know how to behave!"

The word she had chosen to use shocked him. He asked, "Is that what they say in town? That it was murder?"

"Oh, no!" she cried. "No, indeed. They think it's very

89

funny. A man is dead and it's a great big joke. You're by way of being a hero. The sheriff isn't even going to arrest you, although he wanted to; apparently the joke is on Anchor in some way and arresting you would just make it worse. Everybody thinks it's simply hilarious. Oh, this bloodthirsty country!" she gasped. "I know I shouldn't be surprised at anything that happens here. Well, aren't you going to say something?"

Parrish said softly, "Why, if that's the way you feel, Caroline, there's nothing much to say, is there? If you believe I'd kill a man unless it was forced on me—"

"And what about your promise to me?" she cried. "The night we— The other night you promised me faithfully that you'd ride to Anchor the next morning and tell Mr. Wilkison you'd sell at his price! What happened to that promise, honey? Were you so busy fighting with guns that you forgot all about it?"

He said, "Caroline, I regret—"

"*Regret!*" she gasped. "Now there's a real nice word, honey, *regret!* You told me you were going to sell this ranch and take me out of this horrible country; and I believed you and let you—let you— And now you *regret!*" She flushed under his scrutiny. His silence seemed to infuriate her; she tugged at her glove in a blind sort of way; it came off and fell to the floor of the buggy unheeded. Then the ring from her finger made a glinting arc in the sunlight and landed in the dust at his feet. "*There! That's what you want now, isn't it? You want it back, now that you've had everything else!*"

Parrish did not speak, and she began to cry terribly. He looked down at the ring, shining dully in the dust, and knew that, had he loved this girl, he would have picked it up and marched away, regretting each step, because a man could not allow the woman he loved to use that love as a club against him. He would have walked off, hoping and praying that she would call him back. But now he did not know what to do.

Caroline glanced at him furtively, and he saw the quick fear in her eyes as he made no move toward the ring on the ground. It made him ashamed of both of them: of her for making the cheap and melodramatic gesture and of himself for turning it against her by his inaction. He knew suddenly that he could not leave her like this. She had been strength and light and courage to him during the long hard months of his convalescence; he had taken from her more than a man had a right to accept from any woman. It he had once seen something in her that was not there, that was his fault and not hers.

He bent down and picked up the ring and, finding her uncovered left hand, replaced the ring upon the proper finger. After a moment her hand closed over his and her small face looked up at him despairingly, streaked with tears; then, apparently reassured by his expression, she was smiling and blinking the tears quickly from her eyes, suddenly pretty again. She leaned forward and turned up her lips to be kissed.

"I'm sorry, honey!" she gasped, clinging to him. "I don't know what makes me act like. . . . You know I'd love you anywhere, don't you?" It was a victory, but he was not proud of it. He felt the quick, warm pressure of her lips again, and the touch of her hand. Then she sat up quickly, feeling of her bonnet and her hair. "I declare, I must look a sight! You run up and talk to George while I fix myself up. . . . Johnny?"

"Yes?"

"When will I . . . see you again?" she whispered.

He hesitated. "I don't know, Caroline. None of us is riding anywhere alone until we see what Anchor's going to do. I hope Wilkison will let things ride along as they are now, but I'm taking no chances for a while."

"Well," she said, "be careful, honey, but come as soon as you can." Her eyes, that had hated him so recently, held an invitation and a promise now.

When Parrish came into the house, George Menefee was sitting in the largest chair in the living-room, absorbed in the latest copy of the New York newspaper Parrish received regularly in the mail. Unobserved for the moment, Parrish studied this large, dark, pale, and quite handsome young man thoughtfully, finding something illuminating in Menefee's hungry interest in stale news from the East.

There were rumors that the young lawyer's well-to-do parents had shipped their son out here because of certain scandals involving gambling and women. This was the kind of rumor the Basin would be apt to produce about any personable young man from the East with an unexplained income—Menefee certainly did not live and drink and gamble on the proceeds from his tiny law practice—but in this case the story had a ring of plausibility.

Presently Menefee looked up and put the newspaper hastily aside, as if aware that his interest in it had betrayed him in some way. He rose to his feet.

"Your cook makes a fine cup of coffee," he said. "Much obliged. Did you settle your differences with Caroline?"

"I think everything's straightened out," Parrish said. "You take a great interest in my relationship to Caroline, don't you, George?"

"I take a great interest in Caroline," Menefee said, with undeniable dignity. "I did before you came along. There is no secret about it. I would take her away from you if I could." He grinned. "Well, as I said, much obliged. I have to run over to Box Seven. Silas Purdue wants me to draw up some kind of a legal document. There's a client I could do without, if I had enough clients that I could afford to spare one. Half a day's drive, and an argument about my fee at the end of it."

A few minutes later, Parrish watched the buggy drive away. Caroline waved as the vehicle rolled into the last visible bend of the road. Parrish waved back, turned to speak to McCloud, and so caught the queer, cold look on the older man's face. He realized, for the first time, that his foreman had no use at all for the girl he was going to marry. This seemed like an unnecessary complication to an already complicated tangle of human relationships, and instead of speaking, Parrish turned and went into the house. He was working on the ranch accounts when a wagon rolled into the yard. Sighing, he put down the pen, found his hat, and went down the path to find McCloud talking to a large man in overalls whose mouth was a firm slit in a heavily bearded face.

"This is Bud Hinkleman's dad, Mr. Parrish," McCloud

said. "He's come to get his boy's things."

Parrish looked at the stranger disconcerted, not knowing what greeting to expect; but Mr. Hinkleman held out a large calloused hand and said, "Pleased to meet you, Mr. Parrish."

"I am sorry—"

The bearded man shook his head quickly. "Do not blame yourself for something that was not your doing, Mr. Parrish. We all know where the responsibility lies, for this as for most bad things that happen in this valley." He was silent for a moment, then went on: "The lad was bound he was going to be a cowboy. I reckon a farmer's life looked kind of dull to him."

Parrish said, "He was doing the job of a full-grown man here."

"He was a good, hardworking boy, but he had some romantic notions in his head, unlike his brothers," Mr. Hinkleman said. "I put no obstacles in his way, knowing that was no way to cure him. Herding cattle is as honest a way of earning a living as any other, I reckon, although there's some down our way who would dispute that, having had their share of trouble with cattlemen. . . . Well, your foreman has been most kind. I will not keep you any longer, Mr. Parrish."

Parrish said, "We haven't had a chance yet to ride up to the line cabin where it happened. Bud had most of his gear up there with him. The place was burned, but if we find anything we'll send it to you."

"I'd take it as a favor," Mr. Hinkleman said.

"And you'll want this," Parrish said. He unbuckled the gun-belt he was wearing about his waist, wrapped it carefully about the holstered revolver, and held it out. "I took the liberty of borrowing it, having none of my own, but it belonged to your son."

The farmer looked at the weapon, but made no move to take it. "Yes, I remember now, he saved up his money to buy it. It's one of the new Colt guns. He was bound he was going to have it. A fine weapon, but—" Mr. Hinkleman hesitated. "Keep it, Mr. Parrish. It seems that you know how to use it, and there is no one on the farm who

93

could say as much. I think Bud would have liked you to have it. He always spoke well of you to us."

Parrish was silent for a moment. "Thank you," he said at last, and fastened the weapon about him again.

The older man frowned, seeming to examine an idea that had come into his mind. Presently he said, "We're farmers, Mr. Parrish. We're not accustomed to violence; we resort to it only reluctantly, when we are forced to do so."

"I'm hardly a professional gunman myself," Parrish said carefully. "I'm not even much of a cattleman, I'm afraid."

"That is why I can speak to you," Mr. Hinkleman said. "Your neighbor, Mr. Purdue, would not tolerate me on his place or listen to me. Even Mr. McCloud here has a prejudice against any man who wears a bib on his overalls." The bearded man smiled briefly, and stopped smiling. "Mr. Parrish, I still have four sons left to me, and there are seven families besides ours now settled at the South Meadows, each with at least one able-bodied man. If the time should come when a few extra men with guns. . . . Well, you might remember that I spoke to you. Of course, we would want some assurances that after this trouble was settled, we would be left alone to raise our crops in peace. Some agreement could be worked out about fences and water rights. This valley is big enough for all of us, if people would only deal reasonably with each other."

"I have never questioned that," Parrish said. He studied the bearded face of Mr. Hinkleman, conscious that the man's shrewd eyes were watching him in turn. He said carefully, "I'm as averse to violence as you, Mr. Hinkleman. I certainly hope there'll be no further need for it. But if there should be, I'll keep in mind what you've told me."

Mr. Hinkleman nodded slowly, still watching Parrish as if his judgment of the younger man was not quite complete. Then he held out his hand again, smiling his thin-lipped, bearded smile. "Well, it has been pleasant making your acquaintance, Mr. Parrish, after hearing about you. Perhaps we have not been as neighborly as we should, not knowing how we would be received. If you should have occasion to ride down our way, my wife and I would take it kindly if you would pay us a visit."

15

■ The following morning, Parrish took McCloud and DeRosa and rode up to the line cabin where Bud Hinkleman had lost his life. There was nothing to be salvaged from the charred foundations, from which a little smoke still rose. The three men put an end to this with water from the near-by creek and made sure that no pockets of combustion remained, possibly to creep out of the ruins and fire the near-by timber with disastrous results to Rafter H's summer range.

Riding homeward again, they followed the plain trail down Nelly's Canyon—actually a shallow and thinly forested valley—until the distant sound of a shot to the southward made them all draw rein simultaneously, as if at a command. They sat silent, listening. The single report was followed by a quick string of shots from a lighter gun than that which had fired first.

McCloud, ahead of Parrish on the trail, made a disparaging sound. "That last fellow's just pumping lead around; he ain't hitting a damn thing."

This was Parrish's own judgment; but the sound of the first shot, never repeated, remained in his memory uneasily. He said, "Sounds like trouble over on Box Seven."

Joe DeRosa said, "Well, what are we waiting for?" and swung his horse off the trail.

"Hold it, Joe," Parrish said. He frowned at the high ridge to the south, the direction from which the gunshot sounds had reached them; then he glanced at the backbone of the San Luis Hills behind them and at the open reaches of the Basin to the west, visible through the notch of the valley ahead. Ignoring DeRosa's impatience, he turned to the foreman. "Jim, if you were traveling from Box Seven to Anchor, which way would you go?"

McCloud gave the question careful attention. "Why, it depends, Captain," he said after some thought. "Night-times I'd take the road, unless I was in a big hurry and didn't want to meet anybody, in which case I'd cut across our place and pick up the trail at Hard Creek. Daytimes, now, I'd do the same unless I was feeling real shy about being seen, in which case I'd keep to the Hills until I was north of Boundary Creek, and then cut west across the Basin to Anchor."

Parrish said, "That's about the way I figured it."

"Of course," the older man said, "this shooting may have nothing to do with Anchor at all. One of Silas Pur-due's hands maybe jumped a stranger making off with a couple of steers, and there's no telling which way he'd run for it."

Parrish said, "It's possible, and that's all right, too. If it's nothing to do with Anchor, it's nothing to do with us. Silas can take care of any stray rustlers without our help." He turned his horse in the trail. "But let's just make a guess that it's some Wilkison riders, and take a chance on their feeling shy enough to stick to the Hills. Maybe we can cut them off back up the canyon and find out what's going on. I didn't like the sound of that first shot."

"It sure as hell was no saddle-gun," McCloud agreed. "Buffalo rifle, by the sound of it."

Parrish said, "They used them on other targets besides buffalo, where I heard them."

There were no more shots to the southward as they followed the canyon back up through the timber past the burned shell of the line cabin. At last McCloud stopped his horse and indicated a dim path crossing the trail they were following.

"Old Indian trail runs north along this side of the Hills," he said. "It'd be my guess, Captain, if I had to guess."

"We'll gamble on it," Parrish said, and looked around.

96

"We can wait up there in the pines.".

They found shelter for the horses behind a shoulder of the rock that was beginning to show bare here and there at this altitude, and settled down among the trees to wait, watching the trail crossing. From where he lay, Parrish could see a wedge of the Basin spread out before him, framed by the canyon walls, steeper up here than they had been below. In the other direction, looking up through the pines, he could see the naked summits above timber line.

"And they call them hills!" he said softly.

McCloud chuckled beside him and whispered, "You should pay a visit to the Big Guns over to the other side of the Basin, if you want to see real mountains. There's peaks over there no man's ever climbed, and lakes nobody's fished. There's creeks with gold nuggets as big as your fist, so they say. Personally, I never managed to locate one, but I sure tried like hell when I first come to this country, before I learned that cattle was an easier living."

"It's a fine country," Parrish said. "A man's got room to breathe."

"No matter how much room some people have, they always want more, Captain."

"I hope you're wrong," Parrish said. "I certainly hope you're wrong, Jim."

It was very quiet and peaceful where he lay, but he could not help the feeling, intensified by McCloud's words, that this was the uneasy peace of tomorrow's battlefield. Time passed very slowly. Presently he heard sounds of movement close at hand and looked around, annoyed, to see that DeRosa had sat up to roll himself a cigarette. McCloud had noticed the action and was looking at Parrish with a question in his eyes. Parrish shook his head.

McCloud whispered, "Put it away, Joe. Tobacco smell carries a long way."

The younger rider glanced at Parrish for confirmation, muttered something under his breath, tucked the makings back into his shirt pocket, and lay down again beside his rifle.

"Ah, hell," he said to nobody in particular. "This makes

no sense. They could have headed anywhere in the Basin."

McCloud said, "Son, I've got a lot more meat still-hunting than I ever did wearing out my rear end riding after it, and I hunted for an army post up north for a spell. Picking a likely-looking game trail and waiting for something to come along is a damn sight better than crashing through the brush scaring everything within five miles. Right, Captain?"

Parrish nodded and started to speak, but the sound of a shot cut him off. They all looked up, surprised by the closeness of the report; it seemed to come from just across the ridge to the south.

"There's your buffalo gun again, Jim," Parrish said. As he spoke, a lighter weapon fired three times very rapidly and was answered not only by the heavy rifle but by at least two other guns as well. This outburst died away, leaving a few seconds of ringing silence; then the big rifle fired once. There was no answer. Half a minute later, it fired again. Parrish picked up his gun and got to his feet. "Let's go," he said. "That marksman's got somebody pinned down and is holding them while his friends work in close for the kill. We'd better get over there."

The report of the big rifle came to them at varying intervals as they climbed the faint trail—winding back and forth across the face of the canyon wall—as fast as the horses could manage. Reaching the crest, they looked down into the next valley. It was heavily timbered directly below them, but the head of it, to the left, was an open, grassy, bowl-shaped meadow dotted with brushes and large granite boulders. Studying the scene, Parrish noticed first the dead horse, a small brown patch some hundred yards beyond the edge of the timber. Then he caught sight of movement among a cluster of rocks near by and made out the figure of a man crouching there in what seemed to be rather poor cover surrounded by an expanse of open meadow.

"That lad's got himself into a pretty pickle," Parrish said softly to McCloud. "Looks like he let himself be lured out into the open, following the first bunch, and had his horse shot out from under him. Where——?"

As he spoke, a little white point of smoke appeared beside a great boulder near the head of the meadow; seconds later the sound of the shot reached them.

"There he is," McCloud said. "If we sneak up along the ridge here we can get behind him, Captain."

Parrish shook his head. "There's no time. Look in the woods; there's a man working into position below, and judging by the shooting a while back there ought to be another one somewhere around. They'll drive our friend out into the open and finish him off before we can get there, if we try anything fancy. The only thing we can do now is break it up."

He pulled his carbine from the scabbard, cocked it, and fired into the air as he urged his horse down the slope. After a moment he heard his companions come after him, yelling and shooting. Over a mile away he saw the man in the rocks look around quickly at the noise. The man in the timber stood up, hesitated there a moment, perhaps balancing in his mind the importance of his mission against the distance separating him from his horse. He turned and vanished among the pines. On the near side of the meadow a man suddenly appeared out of a small gully; he fired once, wildly, at the approaching riders and ran for the head of the meadow. The man in the rocks fired three times; on the third shot the running man fell on his face and lay still.

The rifleman at the head of the meadow was shooting steadily, Parrish heard a heavy bullet go by quite near, although the range seemed incredible; another kicked up dust directly in front of him, causing his horse to swerve violently. It seemed strange and unpleasant to be under fire again, after the years that had passed. Then the heavy gun was silent and Parrish saw a small man in a fringed buckskin shirt dart from the shelter of the boulder and disappear among the rocks above. A moment later he came into sight again, mounted, driving his horse wildly up the slope; presently he was gone over the ridge to the north, followed, a minute or so later, by the man who had been in the timber.

The Rafter H men rode past the dead horse, whose

former rider rose from his shelter to greet them. Parrish recognized Silas Purdue's foreman, whose name was Lenhart, a spare, balding, middle-aged man with a look of strain on his face.

"Thanks," he said. "Reckon I owe you boys considerable. That damn sharpshooter had me pinned down here like a chicken on a spit; my own damn fault for being careless. I reckon I kind of lost my head for a while there, chasing them." His eyes narrowed with remembered shock. "They got the old man," he said.

"Mr. Purdue?" Parrish asked, startled.

Lenhart nodded. "One bullet through the heart from half a mile away; he never knew what hit him. He's back there a ways. I'd be obliged if you'd lend me a hand with bringing him in." He glanced at the ridge over which the little man in buckskin had fled. "I'll meet up with that fellow later, some day when he hasn't got the range on me by three hundred yards."

16

■ It was well after noon when they rode into the yard at Rafter H, grimly silent, with the memory of Mrs. Purdue's grief fresh in their minds. About to dismount, Parrish checked himself abruptly, watching Wash Breed come out of the barn, leading a tall chestnut gelding of finer breeding than was usually seen around Rafter H or any of the other ranches in the valley, except one. The old rider stopped in front of him.

"You've got a visitor waiting for you up at the house, Captain," he said in a carefully expressionless voice. "Been waiting right some time. As a matter of fact, she'd just given you up and asked me to get her horse out for her. I'd put it in the barn, since she seemed not to favor having it standing around in plain sight."

Parrish nodded, swung himself out of the saddle, and walked to the pump in the yard, stripping off his shirt. One of the men worked the pump for him as he washed off the soot and dust he had picked up on the ride; somebody heaved him a towel from the bunkhouse as he straightened up, gasping from the shock of the cold water. He put the shirt back on and looked about for his hat. McCloud gave it to him.

"Watch yourself," the foreman said softly. "There's more ways of getting a man than putting an ounce of lead through his chest with a buffalo rifle. There are guns in the house and she's a Wilkison. Don't forget it, son."

"I'm not likely to forget it," Parrish said. He turned and strode up the path.

She was standing in the center of the room, facing the door, when he entered. They confronted each other in silence for a time. He made note of her appearance; she was wearing a modestly full, dark green, divided riding skirt, and a boy's wool shirt, open at the throat. Her thick brown hair needed the touch of a comb; it was, he thought, a sign of youth and inexperience. No grown woman would have waited so long for a man—even a man she despised —without taking advantage of the opportunity to make this small adjustment to her appearance.

Judith Wilkison said sharply, "I was just about to leave."

"Yes, Wash told me."

"Wash? Is that the man's name? The nice, old one."

"Yes," Parrish said. "Wash Breed."

"He said you'd be back before noon or I wouldn't have waited."

"We expected to."

She hesitated. "What happened? Did you . . . did you have any trouble?"

He studied her face for a moment. Then he grimaced and pushed a hand across his mouth as if to rub the expression away. He said, "I don't wish to seem inhospitable,

101

Miss Wilkison, but you've picked a poor time to pay us a call. My neighbor, Silas Purdue, was shot from ambush a few hours ago. We're kind of expecting trouble of a similar nature here."

The tall girl in front of him seemed to sway. "Mr. Purdue?" After a while she whispered, "Is he—?"

Parrish nodded. "Quite dead."

"Then—" She licked her lips. "Then I came to the wrong place. But I was so sure—" Her voice trailed off.

"You knew?" Parrish asked. She inclined her head. He said flatly, expressing neither belief nor disbelief, "And you came to warn us."

She turned abruptly away from him. Presently she said in a stiff voice, "The man you want is about five feet five, a greasy little man who wears a fringed buckskin shirt. They call him Sniper Boone. He used to be a buffalo hunter, until he found he could make more money with his gun—in other ways. He was sighting a big Sharps rifle in back of the ranch this morning. I never saw anybody shoot like that before. Cole saw me watching and said it was a bet of some kind. He paid the man two hundred dollars and promised him three hundred later."

Parrish said deliberately, "Hansen picks his tools well. That Kid fellow for the sheriff, this sharpshooter for old Silas. It makes me kind of wonder what he has in mind for me." He made his voice suddenly harsh: "Why don't you go back home, Miss Wilkison, and tell him he'd better stick to using men for the work?"

It brought her around to face him again, quite pale. She started to speak indignantly, and checked herself, watching him. A little frown came to her face. He saw her anger die as she probed for his motives for insulting her; then her eyes showed a glint of amusement and she said, "You don't believe that."

He grinned faintly. "Well, I have to keep the possibility in mind, don't I?"

"You're not as gentle as you look, Mr. Parrish," she murmured.

"My looks have been a handicap as long as I can remember," he said. "I used to dream of being six feet tall

102

and weighing two hundred pounds and being able to whale the tar out of anybody who called me Red. . . . What are you laughing at?"

"Dreams are funny things, I guess," she said. "Personally, I always dream of being about six inches shorter and lots prettier—"

She broke off, coloring, as if ashamed of having betrayed herself to him. They faced each other in silence for a moment, and Parrish found himself looking at her narrowly, with an odd sense of discovery, seeing the fine shape of her face, and the nice line of her throat, and the pleasant way she had of standing and talking to a man, unself-consciously, without posing or fidgeting. It annoyed him that she should want to change herself in any way. *Why*, he thought, *why, she's beautiful*. The thought, slipping into his mind like that, startled him immeasurably.

His expression must have betrayed him, for he saw her color deepen as if his regard was embarrassing her; then a puzzled, almost frightened look came into her eyes, as if she, too, had made an unexpected discovery. She started to speak impulsively. Parrish turned away.

"You had no business coming here, Miss Wilkison!" he said roughly. "You probably meant well, but it was a foolish thing to do. I suggest you leave now, before your presence makes trouble for everybody concerned, including yourself."

She was silent for a while behind him. At last she asked quietly, "Is that what you want?"

He swung back to look at her. "We can't always have what we want, Miss Wilkison. A man—" He cleared his throat. "A man has certain obligations and commitments that he has to honor."

"Honor is a nice word," she said. "It's not much in use among women, though, Mr. Parrish." She smiled. "I'm sorry. You're right; I shouldn't have come. It was a silly idea. I just thought. . . . Honor and loyalty are very grand, Mr. Parrish, but there comes a time when—when one has to try to do something to stop—" She shivered and drew a long breath. "Are you going to try to fight Anchor, Mr. Parrish?"

"I'll be here. If that means fighting, I'll fight, as I told your father a couple of nights ago."

She shook her head quickly. "You're a fool to try it. You don't know what it's like, living at Anchor now; you don't know the kind of men. . . . All the old hands, who were nice to me and played with me when I was a little girl and taught me to ride and rope and shoot, they're all gone now except Phil Bennett, and he's not going to put up with it much longer. It's like living with a wolf-pack now; and they're all Cole's men. Dad doesn't realize it yet, but Anchor isn't his ranch any longer. Cole just pretends to consult with him. And Martha—she's fooling herself as much as Dad is. Cole's convinced them both that he can make Anchor the greatest ranch in the territory. Well, maybe he can, but any fool can see whose ranch it's going to be. But *they* won't see it. It's been Dad's dream for so long, and Martha's so ambitious, they both close their eyes to—" She checked herself. "But that's beside the point. I've picked a damn poor place to come for sympathy, haven't I? Almost as poor as the place you chose to look for peace the other night. The point is that Cole has between thirty and forty riders to throw against you, Mr. Parrish, and he can get more if he needs them."

Parrish said, "He'll need them."

She flushed a little. "Why, you're as arrogant in your way as he is in his!"

Parrish said, "Miss Wilkison, it's not arrogant to know your own capabilities. I've done some fighting, remember; and when I say that I can hold this ranch against anything short of a disciplined military force, I'm not making an empty boast, I'm stating a cold fact. I can do it, and I know precisely how I'm going to do it, and it will be the meanest, dirtiest fighting Cole Hansen ever saw in his life. No civilized person will want to shake hands with me when I'm through, but I'll be sitting right here on Rafter H when the smoke clears." He drew a breath. "And as for you, there is nothing for you here but danger, Miss Wilkison. I suggest that in the future you stay on your own side of the fence. It's nothing to me if your father is tricked by the man he was fool enough to hire, or your sister by the

104

man she was fool enough to marry. I'm sorry for you, but there's obviously nothing I can do about it, and my sympathy will not keep me from pulling your home down around your ears should Cole Hansen give me cause to strike back at him. Is that clear?"

She studied his face for a moment before she nodded minutely. Then she picked up her hat, went to the door, and turned. "It's quite clear, Mr. Parrish," she said. "To me. I hope it's just as clear to you."

"What do you mean?"

"I mean, I hope you fight as tough as you talk, Mr. Parrish. Don't let any sympathy for me get in your way; you don't owe me a damn thing."

He watched her turn and walk swiftly across the porch and down the steps. Halfway down the path, she began to run. He watched her fling herself onto the horse Wash Breed had brought out for her and set off around the base of the knoll at a gallop. He walked slowly around the house to follow her swift progress, seeing the small figure of horse and rider presently vanish into the arroyo of Hard Creek and shortly thereafter emerge on the higher ground beyond, going at last out of sight into the broken country to the north. He stood there until the vague regret in his mind became too strong and too clear and too close to taking a recognizable form that, he knew, would seriously endanger his peace of mind. Then he swung himself around and busied himself with making a tour of inspection around the house that presently brought him back to the point at which he had started.

Standing there—the girl almost, but not quite, out of his mind now—he squinted down the hillside in a preoccupied way and found his imagination turning the hot afternoon sunshine to darkness—at best pale moonlight—and peopling the slopes with dim and hostile shapes. With memory to help him, he had no trouble in visualizing the intermittent flashes of the attackers' guns, or in imaging the cracking sound of rifle fire; bullets would be smashing into the logs of the house and finding entry by the windows. . . .

Parrish frowned, letting a thought move into his mind:

I cannot put six good men into a crackerbox for thirty men to shoot at. No ranch is worth it. Besides, even an impregnable fortress was all very well in its way, but it necessarily had certain qualities in common with a prison, in particular the fact that under certain conditions the inmates might have considerable difficulty in getting out. He stood for a moment longer looking bleakly to the north, the direction Judith Wilkison had taken, and the direction from which the attack would come. Then he turned on his heel and shouted for McCloud, who appeared close at hand, as if he had been awaiting the summons.

"Tell the men to get their gear together," Parrish said. "Provisions for a week and all the ammunition we have on the place. We're moving out."

17

■ At the gate, Parrish paused to look back up at the house, which looked empty and forlorn in the growing twilight. Both the front door and the kitchen door hung carelessly open and no light burned inside; no smoke rose from the chimney. A book with a broken cover lay open on the porch, its pages ruffled by the evening breeze, and along the steep path lay odd scraps of paper, a soiled kitchen towel, a tangle of cord, a dented saucepan, and a man's sock: the kind of debris the inhabitants of a house would drop as they moved out in a hurry, taking only their most essential belongings with them. Across the yard, the bunkhouse had the same hastily evacuated look. Even the barn managed in some way to look deserted, giving, Parrish thought wryly, the impression that even the rats had packed up and left.

He turned to look up at the men awaiting him, already mounted. He spoke to Jackson and Harry Germack. "All right, you two can get going. I doubt that you'll have any business, but we can't afford to take a chance of missing them entirely." As the two riders started away from him, he checked them with his voice, harshly; "Remember your instructions. If they do come your way, do your job fast and pull out immediately. You're not being paid to get yourselves killed."

He watched them take off up the road in the fading twilight, disappearing around the curve from which Caroline had waved good-by to him yesterday.

He said, "Well, I guess there's no more to be done here."

He swung aboard the mount that had been saddled for him, the small, white-footed mare that he often rode. She needed no urging, and they set off to the north without looking back at the ranch lying dark and deserted behind them in the gathering dusk. Wash Breed was waiting for them when they emerged from the arroyo of Hard Creek onto the higher ground beyond.

"Not a sign from them anywhere," he reported. "I've been halfway up to Boundary Creek and back. If there's a man on the upper range, he's six feet under the ground." After a moment, he added with a jerk of his head, "There's a gully over that way that'll do for the horses."

Parrish said, "All right, Wash. But let's first get this operation worked out while we still have a little light. What about it, Jim?"

Directly challenged, McCloud said grimly, "I still think it's a fool idea, Captain. Leaving the ranch and splitting up the men like this—"

Parrish said wearily, "We've been through all that, Jim."

"You don't even know when they're going to hit us! Or where."

"It stands to reason they're going to hit us where they expect to find us, which means the ranch. Hansen isn't going to waste time on the stock, which is the only other thing he could hit. He's started the ball rolling by having Silas Purdue killed; now he's got to take care of us fast, hoping to catch us off balance; otherwise he'll have a range war on his hands that may drag on long enough to raise a stink that he can't afford. If he doesn't come tonight he'll come tomorrow night; but I doubt that he'll wait that long. As for splitting the men up, four's all we can use here; the others might as well be posted where they can do some good."

McCloud shook his head stubbornly. "Even granting that you've got Hansen figured right, Captain, it seems a damn fool thing to leave the house, which is as good as a fort, to go fighting in the open."

Parrish said, "Look, Jim, Hansen knows all about our house. If he comes at all—and I think he will—he'll come prepared either to blast us out or starve us out. There's never anything to be gained by fighting an enemy on his own terms, particularly when he outnumbers you five to one."

"Well, how the hell do you know he's going to come this way when he doesn't find us at the ranch?"

"Why, it's the quickest way home for him. He'll make his approach carefully, all right, expecting to find us alerted by Mr. Purdue's death. But when he finds an empty house, with every sign that we've lit out in a panic—"

"All right, Captain," McCloud said stiffly. "All right. It's your ranch. You're the boss. Tell us what to do and we'll do it."

Parrish did not like the unconvinced sound of the older man's voice; it emphasized his own doubts. But there was always something to be said against any plan, and grim experience had taught him to abide by his own decisions. There was nothing worse than an officer who couldn't keep his mind made up.

He said crisply, "We'll dig in along the hillside there. Pick your places now so you can find them after dark; then Wash will take the horses to cover, and the rest of us will pull back behind the ridge in case Hansen should be foolhardy enough to make his approach this way, which isn't likely. If he should come, we'll let him go through and take him on his way home, when he'll be more off his guard. Is that understood?"

Up on the ridge, the breeze was quite cool. Presently

108

the darkness was complete. The ground upon which he lay was hard and uneven, and his gun-belt and the spare rifle cartridges with which his pockets were burdened made it difficult for Parrish to settle himself comfortably. . . . He opened his eyes suddenly to a shocked realization that, worn out by the long day, he had fallen asleep. There was something frighteningly familiar about this; it was as if he had slipped back into a set of habits that he thought he had discarded and forgotten. During the war he had been able to sleep anywhere; afterward, sleep had not always been so easy to find. There was light in the sky now and his heart beat heavily before he realized that it was only the cold light of the moon.

". . . asleep?" someone was saying softly beside him. "Well, I reckon you've got to give the dude credit for that much. Damned if I could sleep." This was Joe DeRosa's voice.

McCloud's voice replied, "Hell, there's nothing wrong with the boy's nerve; it's just his good sense I'm worrying about."

"Boy, hell," DeRosa said irritably. "He's older than I am. But damn if it doesn't go against the grain to take orders from a baby-faced dude I could break apart with one hand. What does he know about this kind of business, anyway?"

"That's something we'll soon find out," McCloud murmured.

"Maybe," the younger man said. "But the moon's up and nothing's happened. I'd say we get no visitors tonight."

Parrish stirred, to warn them that he was awake, and they fell silent. He sat up cautiously, and frowned at the asymmetrical face of the moon, hanging well clear of the ridge above him.

"Nothing yet?"

"Even the coyotes are home in bed," DeRosa said. "I wish I was. Well, I'll get back up on top."

"I'll spell you a while," McCloud offered.

"Stay where you are," the younger man said. "I've got me a soft spot all broke in."

They listened to his retreating footsteps until the sound

died away. Parrish frowned at the sky above him, thinking that DeRosa was a disciplinary problem that would have to be solved sooner or later. He listened, but there was nothing to hear.

"Jim," he said softly.

The foreman stirred, not far away. "What is it, Captain?"

"Cole Hansen carries a peculiar kind of gun. It has no trigger. What's the advantage of that?"

McCloud turned his head to study his employer; there was a pause before he spoke, as if he were considering all possible implications of the question. "Yeh, I heard he was a slipgun artist," he said at last. "Why, that's a gun rigged for fanning the hammer, Captain; or for a single shot you just haul her back and let her slip out from under. Harder to shoot straight at any distance than a regular pistol, but a hell of a lot faster if you want to ventilate a saloon in a hurry. When you see a gun like that you can generally figure the man packing it is best left alone. It's not a weapon you'd pick for shooting jackrabbits."

Parrish frowned at the information, trying to find some meaning in it. "I just wondered," he said. "I never came across a gun like that in the army. Then you'd say that Hansen was by way of being a professional gunman?"

"Well, I wouldn't care to go up against him myself," the foreman admitted wryly. "I'm frank to admit that he's out of my class; and I'd say he was out of yours, too, Captain, in spite of the way you took care of that Kid fellow. . . . As for being professional, I have no doubt that a couple of years back, if you wanted a man killed, you could probably slip Hansen a hundred dollars and he'd do the job for you. I wouldn't say it was the way he made his living, but he wouldn't turn the money down. The story is that he pulled out of Kansas right after the war like a lot of other quick-trigger boys; then he's supposed to've done some fighting below the border and kind of stage-managed a range war down in Texas, after which he put the fear of God into a couple of mining towns that were supposed to be death on marshals. That's where Lew Wilkison found him. Lew's been looking for a long time for a man to bust this range open, and I reckon Hansen seemed to fill the bill. Lew brought him here and gave him a free hand. I wouldn't know whether the daughter was part of the bargain or just a wrinkle that Hansen thought up by himself and made the old man swallow."

Parrish asked thoughtfully, "But if Hansen is a gunman in his own right, why would he hire other men to do his shooting for him?"

"That's easy," McCloud said. "He's got big ideas now, Hansen has. This valley looks good to him and he figures to keep on living here. He doesn't want a lot of local killings coming back to plague him later when he's rich and respectable. If you hire a man to do your killing you can always wash your hands of him when the job's done. No, I figure Hansen for a hard, smart man who's finished his hell-raising and picked himself a place for settling down. He's going to be a big rancher now, with a pretty wife and even some kids, give him time; Anchor will be all his one day—"

Parrish said, "According to the girl, it's practically all his already. Well, a Wilkison hired him and a Wilkison married him. What happens at Anchor is none of my concern, except as it affects Rafter H."

He was aware of his foreman glancing at him sharply, as if detecting a false note in this disclaimer. Somewhat annoyed, he was starting to speak again when a rustle of movement and a dislodged pebble announced the return of Joe DeRosa.

"What is it, Joe?" Parrish whispered.

"I thought I saw something moving, over by the ranch."

Parrish and McCloud picked up their rifles and scrambled to the crest of the ridge. From there, the landscape had a cold, dead look in the moonlight; the distant ranch house upon its little knoll was a toy building in a deserted world. Even the group of tiny horsemen making their way cautiously up to the house gave no feeling of life to the scene.

"Well, there they are," McCloud said. "You figured it right so far, Captain, I've got to hand it to you. They must have cut east and crossed the creek back up in the San

111

Loos, figuring we wouldn't expect them from that direction." His voice was low, as if he was afraid it might carry, even at that distance. "There's only half a dozen there," he whispered. "I reckon the rest are holding back——"

Suddenly something changed about the picture they were watching. It was an almost imperceptible change at first, a slight sharpening of the outlines of the house and the surrounding terrain, as if the moonlight had become stronger in this area. Then a faint reddish glow began to work its way upward into the sky.

Joe DeRosa made an incredulous sound in his throat. *"Why, the bastards are burning——"*

Parrish asked softly, "What did you expect them to do, Joe? Give it a fresh coat of paint for us?"

The rider turned his head to stare. McCloud said roughly, "You knew they'd do that, Captain? And you had us pull out——"

Parrish watched a tongue of flame rise into sight, behind and slightly to the right of the house. That would be the barn. "What you seem to forget," he murmured, "is that Anchor controls the law in this neighborhood. Wilkison has powerful friends, clear back to Washington. Give him an excuse and he'll have us outlaws by morning. But I doubt that anybody's going to have the nerve to blame us publicly for anything we do to a gang of men we catch redhanded burning our ranch!"

"There goes the house, now," McCloud whispered.

Suddenly all the windows of the low log building were alight; coal-oil must have been used liberally to cause such instant ignition. Something painful and unfamiliar gripped Parrish's throat as he watched the burning of the place that had been his home for three years. He knew a quick surge of anger, the strength of which surprised him, since he did not consider himself a sentimental man. He had, after all, sacrificed the ranch deliberately, as part of a plan. Yet the actual loss struck him more deeply than he had anticipated, and he looked away, unable to make himself watch the progress of the fire.

Presently McCloud whispered, "They're going for their

horses. Looks like they might be heading this way. Joe, run tell Wash we got company coming."

DeRosa plunged away from them, ducking low as he crossed the skyline; Parrish and McCloud followed after a moment, scrambling down the brushy slope on the far side of the ridge to the positions previously chosen. Parrish settled down behind a scrubby bush—some day, he thought vaguely, he would have to learn a little more about the vegetation of this country he seemed to have adopted—pushed his carbine out ahead of him, and waited for the beating of his heart to subside, but this did not happen. There was still a vague regret in his mind at the step he was about to take; yet there was a savage pleasure to the moment also. This was something a man missed when it went out of his life, a grim and terrible fulfillment that could not be found elsewhere. This was where you staked your life on the turn of the big wheel. Once you had played this game you never forgot it.

The trail below him shone white in the moonlight; the shadows all around him were black. From his position he could still see the glow of the burning ranch. The first tall flames had now died back to a steady fire that would probably last—fed by the heavy logs of the house—until morning and beyond. Even at a distance, the fire gave a hellish and unreal cast to the scene; it was like having an erupting volcano on the horizon.

He could not see McCloud—the foreman seemed to have melted into the hillside on his right—but he heard a whisper from that direction. "Get set. Here they come, Captain."

A faint click reached him and he drew back the hammer of his carbine to full cock. He heard the same small metallic noise repeated twice more along the slope. Then he was watching the riders approaching the far rim of the arroyo in the moonlight. They seemed to dam up like a dark flood at the head of the trail leading down to the creek, along which they could pass only in single file. He could hear voices now, and laughter, and all the little iron and leather noises that attended the movement of a large group of horsemen. The leaders were splashing across the

113

creek before the tail of the column had started down the trail.

Somebody in the line made an audible comment in a voice that held a certain uneasiness, and Cole Hansen's confident reply came clearly over the still air: ". . . . pulled out for good. The dude wanted no part of what happened to Silas Purdue, I reckon. If he'd been going to fight, he'd have done it before we burned him out."

Someone near the rear of the line told a joke that brought a shout of laughter; and there was confusion accompanied by loud curses as a horse abruptly stopped to drink at the creek. All along the line there was a clear sense of relaxation; these were men who had been keyed up for a bloody assault upon a well-defended place and had found the place empty. Parrish knew the feeling exactly; it had happened to him more than once. He could feel the beating of his heart shaking him in a familiar way, and his mouth was dry.

The first rider out of the arroyo checked his horse briefly to look around and make certain his companions were following. He was no one Parrish had ever seen before, a plump man in range garb that looked poorly cared for, even in the moonlight. He sent his mount ahead, and now the next man was in sight; this one was DeRosa's. The third was Wash Breed's and the fourth belonged to Mc-Cloud, whose shot would be the signal.

It came before Parrish was fully expecting it: a sharp, hard, smash of sound from the right; and two more rifles crashed upon the heels of it. A man screamed, and a horse reared and whinnied in panic. Parrish saw his own target look wildly around and drive in his spurs; he checked his first impulsive yank at the trigger and, suddenly cold and steady, watched the rider rush past him and followed with the sights, swung a little ahead, and pressed off gently, letting the piece fire itself when ready. The man went down and the horse, crying in terror, fled away along the trail.

McCloud and Wash Breed were firing steadily now, at spaced, deliberate intervals; DeRosa had got excited and was shooting too fast. Parrish noted this automatically as he threw the lever and recocked his Spencer; he wished for a good sergeant to chew DeRosa's ear off. About to crawl over, he heard Wash Breed speak sharply to the younger rider, whose rate of fire slacked off. Parrish began to fire carefully, aiming low and searching the path and the slopes of the gully with his shots. A riderless horse broke out of the crush at the head of the trail and stampeded past; it was followed by a horseman crouching low and flogging his mount in a desperate attempt to break through the curtain of fire since escape to the rear was blocked. Three rifles found the man simultaneously and smashed him from the saddle.

There was no conscience now, and no remorse and no mercy. *I left the door open,* Parrish thought. *I left the door open, but no one forced you to walk in. Now see how you like your welcome!* The taste of burned powder was in his mouth, and his ears were deafened by the successive reports, his shoulder bruised by the incessant recoil of his weapon. The count he was keeping in the back of his mind warned him when his magazine was running empty; he fired the last shot and came to his feet, seeing McCloud rise up near by, and Breed also. DeRosa was still firing.

"Pry that hothead loose and let's go," Parrish hissed. "On the double now, before they catch their breath!"

A bullet went by overhead with a sound like that of cloth ripped across; another ricocheted from the hillside not far away, glancing skyward with a nasty, quavering sound. They ran for the horses, crouching. The little black mare reared excitedly as Parrish hit the saddle, but this was only part of the wildness of the night and he pulled her down brutally; then they were away. Behind them a single rifle banged repeatedly. This fell silent. Cole Hansen's voice, choked up with rage, bellowed orders.

Presently, riding hard, they heard, over the growing sounds of pursuit, the snapping noise of gunfire in the southwest, and checked their horses briefly to listen. The noise swelled momentarily, and died away. They looked at each other in the moonlight; Parrish saw the wolf-like look on the faces of his companions and knew that the same look was on his own face.

"By God!" DeRosa muttered in an awed, pleased voice,

"by God, I'll bet a bunch of the stragglers was hightailing it home by the road and ran into Harry and Jackson! By God, we caught them coming and going! They won't forget this night in a hurry!"

18

■ The camp was well up in the San Luis hills, in a high canyon where a small, brawling stream tumbled through a series of deep pools. It was a pleasant enough place in which to rest up after three days of hard riding, although Parrish found that he could not relax quite enough to enjoy the sound of the stream, which disturbed him with its hint of hostile voices half covered up. You could listen to a brook and hear anything.

He started up, reaching for his gun, when McCloud sat down beside him. Then he lay back again upon his blankets, looking at the darkening sky overhead, while the foreman made himself a cigarette and lit it. Neither man spoke for a while.

At last Parrish asked, "Is Wash back yet?"

"Not yet."

"I hope he hasn't run into trouble."

"Wash has kept his scalp safe from the Sioux, Comanches, Apaches, and half a dozen other tribes of Indians. It'll take more than a bunch of saloon hardcases to catch that old buzzard."

"How's Harry?" Parrish asked. Harry Germack had been the only casualty so far, creased by a chance bullet fired by an Anchor rider who had stumbled across them on the second day.

"Ah, Harry's all right," McCloud said. "But it sure is a

116

hell of a place for a riding man to get himself hit; he must have been standing up in his stirrups to manage it.."

Parrish said, "It occurs to me that I have overlooked something. I forgot to make a little speech to the effect that any man who wanted to pull out could do so without prejudice."

McCloud chuckled. "Captain, if the boys wanted to drift, they'd drift without being given permission; and missing half a month's pay wouldn't stop them, either. I wouldn't fool around with any speeches; nobody out here pays much heed to them." He smoked for a while. "Quiet today," he said presently. "Didn't sight a rider anywhere, coming here. Seems almost like they'd give up trying."

"It's not likely," Parrish said.

"No," the older man agreed. "Hansen's got a mess of dead and wounded to answer for. We played hell with his bunch, for a fact. He's going to have to get us, if he wants to keep them in hand. Those boys ride for money, and they're not used to taking punishment. If Hansen leads them into another deadfall like that one, they're going to start finding themselves shooting jobs elsewhere, where the bullets don't come back at them so fast."

Parrish said, "That's more or less what I'm counting on. But for the moment it's his move, and I'm wondering what it'll be."

"Well," McCloud said, "he might take a crack at the stock now, figuring that we'd have to come out and fight or be cleaned out."

Parrish said, "Maybe, if he thinks I'm fool enough to risk men for the sake of cattle. Anything he takes from my range I can take back double from his, any time I want to; and he probably knows it. I don't think it'll be the stock." He shrugged his shoulders, looking up at the sky. "Well, we'll see soon enough, I suppose."

The old foreman looked at him curiously. "You take it calm enough, Captain. Here you was about to get married and go back East to raise a family, and instead you're hiding out in the hills with two-three dozen men hunting your hide. Another fellow might act a little upset about having his plans plumb ruined like that."

Parrish glanced at him quickly, started to speak, and stopped. "Ah, go to sleep, Jim," he said, somewhat irritably.

The older man chuckled at some private thought, "Good night, Captain."

Parrish watched him make his way to his blankets and lie down. The camp was quiet except for the occasional clatter of a pan from near the low and almost smokeless fire, where the cook was still working. Presently Jackson crushed out a cigarette, picked up his carbine, and moved off down the canyon toward the lookout point, a shabby, bowlegged man who looked misshapen and awkward off a horse.

A few minutes later, Joe DeRosa, relieved, came back and sat down by the fire to eat, his young, dark, impatient face given a sinister cast by the firelight and a heavy growth of beard. In the past few days, Parrish had come to know all these men quite well. It was a little disconcerting to think that they had, doubtless, also come to know him.

The foreman's words came back to him: "You take it calm enough, Captain." There was truth in the judgment; for a man whose plans for the future had been shattered, whose property had been destroyed, whose very life was in imminent danger, he was feeling quite happy. He recognized the happiness for what it was, the irresponsible pleasure of a small boy playing hooky from school to go fishing.

This was clearly an improper attitude to take toward a grim business in which men were being killed and homes burned to the ground, and certainly he took no pleasure in the deaths he had helped to cause; yet the fact remained that as long as he was engaged in a bitter struggle for existence he could not be expected to pay much attention to more intimate and personal problems. It was a respite of sorts. For the moment, at least, he was free.

Ashamed of the thought, he put it out of his mind, rolled himself into his blankets, and went to sleep. Jackson aroused him at midnight; at four he was relieved by McCloud. He awoke to a gray morning, with a sprinkle of rain that let up after breakfast. By noon the sky was clear and the sun was hot. He was eating lunch when DeRosa reported Wash Breed approaching from below with two companions.

"Two?" Parrish asked, surprised.

"That's right, Captain. That Kruger fellow that's got a ranch a little to the south, and Doc Kinsman."

Parrish frowned. "I wonder what the doctor wants. All right, Joe, thanks."

He rose and watched the newcomers ride into camp. The wiry figure of Dr. Kinsman, in his customary gray suit, looked out of place on the back of a horse; the doctor had never learned to ride well and much preferred his buggy. He dismounted with the assurance of a man who takes his welcome for granted, but his companion remained in the saddle, making no abrupt movements and keeping his hands clasped in plain sight on the horn. It was clear that Tex Kruger had visited the camps of hunted men before; not strange, considering the reputation of these hills.

Parrish moved forward, and the tall, blond Texan looked down at him. "You sent for me, Captain?"

"That's right," Parrish said. "Light down and have something to eat. Where'd you find the doctor?"

"That's a funny thing," Kruger said. "He came riding up in his buggy this morning just as we was setting out; said he was looking for somebody to bring him to you. Has a message for you, I think." The Texan dismounted and grinned, holding out his hand. "I'm mighty glad to see you, Captain; I'd like to shake your hand and ask you to forget what I said last time we met. Why, the blood-pressure over to Anchor is something terrible, they tell me. The old man like to have apoplexy the other morning when they started carting in the wounded; and Cole Hansen's wife won't speak to him, which don't do his disposition any good. And the news of Silas Purdue's will didn't help the situation, either."

They shook hands. Parrish said, "Silas Purdue's will? What about it?"

"Why, it seems that old Silas left Box Seven to you, Mr.

119

Parrish. Leastways, that's the story that's going around the Basin."

Parrish frowned. "It seems unlikely, to say the least," he said. "The last time I saw Mr. Purdue alive, he was telling me never to set foot on his place again."

"That was when he thought you were selling out to Wilkison. But when he heard about your fight with the Pecos Kid, and the way you laid the law down to Anchor that night, well, I reckon he figured Mrs. Purdue wasn't going to be able to hang onto the ranch by herself, if anything happened to him; and he wasn't going to let Anchor have it if he could help it. So he had that lawyer Menefee come out and make him a new will, the day before he was killed."

"So that's what Menefee was on his way out there for that day."

"That's it," the Texan said. "Old man Purdue had himself the last laugh, after all. You got quite a spread now, Captain, if you can hang onto it."

"Yes," Parrish said thoughtfully. "Well, why don't you go over by the fire and have the cook fix you up while I see what's brought Dr. Kinsman all this way?"

He watched Kruger move away from him, weighing the man in his mind; then he turned to face the doctor, who pursed his lips and said, "Well, my boy, you have been raising hell, haven't you?"

Parrish said dryly, "It seems to be a crop that does well in this climate, Dr. Kinsman."

"Three men dead and seven wounded," the doctor said. "That is quite a harvest for one night, even for the Basin. As Tex said, you're not popular at Anchor."

"I was afraid they might be a little provoked with me," Parrish agreed. "But it could not be helped. What brings you here? Not that we aren't glad to see you. Harry Germack's got a bullet-gouge that could use your attention."

The doctor raised his eyebrows. "Is that the only damage?"

"I haven't got enough men that I can afford to let them get shot," Parrish said.

"Cole Hansen claims to have wiped out half your crew."

"He'd have to claim something like that. But he'll have a hard time producing the bodies."

"Um," the doctor said. "Well, I have a message for you. The young lady said that it was desperate and urgent and a matter of life and death. I tried to convince her that I was neither Cupid nor the United States Mail, but—" He shrugged. "It seems that a man never gets quite old enough to be imperious to a pretty girl's tears. Here you are."

He produced a somewhat crumpled envelope. Parrish took it and opened it, aware that everyone in the camp seemed suddenly to have stopped to watch. He drew out the enclosed sheet of paper and studied the three lines of writing it contained. Dr. Kinsman's recital had left him unprepared for the signature, which came as a small surprise, although there was no reason it should have. There was, after all, no other person in the Basin with as much right to write to him. He read the message carefully. *Honey, please come at once. Something dreadful has happened. I must see you right away. Love, Caroline.*

McCloud had come up to stand beside him. Parrish hesitated, because it seemed like a very personal thing to be showing to another man; yet they were all involved in this, and he passed the note across. The foreman glanced at it, frowned, and turned to look at him. "Is there any doubt in your mind that it's a trick, Captain?"

Parrish did not speak at once. His first reaction, of which he was not proud, had been the instinctive, trapped feeling that, he supposed, any man would have upon receiving an urgent, veiled, and desperate message from a girl to whom he had recently made love. Now, he retrieved the note and reread it thoughtfully. "You think Hansen's behind it, Jim?"

"What else? It's his move, like we was talking about last night. He's got hold of Miss Vail and forced her to write you; he'll be waiting if you're fool enough to ride in."

"But—" Parrish checked himself, still studying the note uneasily. He could not tell another man that this was precisely the kind of note that Caroline would write if she had made a certain discovery. Hansen, on the other hand, would not be so vague; he would want time and place clearly established, if he were baiting a trap. Yet it was possible that the man was more subtle than he had seemed. Parrish glanced at Dr. Kinsman, who shook his head to indicate that he was reluctant to express an opinion upon which men's lives might hang.

"I can't tell you, John," he said. "All I can say is that the little girl seemed distressed and afraid. She asked me to tell you to be careful; she repeated that several times. She said for me to tell you to be real sure you didn't take any chances for her sake."

McCloud slapped his thigh triumphantly. "What more do you want, Captain? She was trying to warn you as much as she dared, that's clear enough. Hansen was probably holding a gun on her folks' or threatening to mark her with a branding iron if she didn't act right."

Parrish said, "In which case, Jim, she's apt to be in real trouble if I don't turn up. Hansen will know she passed us the warning."

"Ah, listen, son, I know how you feel, but there's no sense committing suicide; even the seven of us wouldn't stand a chance. He'll be set and ready for us."

"Who said anything about committing suicide?" Parrish asked softly. There was a growing rage inside him at the thought of Caroline in Hansen's hands; somehow, the fact that he was no longer in love with her made the situation more unbearable than it would otherwise have been. It was something else he owed her, that she should not have to suffer fear and indignity for his sake. He drew a long breath. "And who said anything about seven men? Mr. Kruger—" He swung about to face the Texan. "Mr. Kruger, you once said something about these hills being full of men who could ride and shoot and were willing to do both for the sake of being left alone. How many can you produce, and how soon?"

Kruger chewed deliberately, swallowed, and rose to his feet, still holding the plate from which he had been eating. He showed no surprise at the question. "Why, I reckon I can have a dozen for you by nightfall, Captain; four or five more if you're not choosy about their reputations."

"I can't afford to be choosy," Parrish said. "Just so you keep them in hand. . . . I'll head down to South Meadows and have a talk with that farmer, Hinkleman," he went on. "He ought to be able to scrape up half a dozen men with some kind of guns. I'll stop by Box Seven on the way and send along any of the Purdue hands that are still around."

McCloud chuckled. "Why, we'll be able to match Hansen gun for gun, and then some. He's got less than thirty still on their feet, and he'll have left a few to guard the ranch. We'll bust his little trap wide open—"

Parrish said grimly, "Jim, you'll never be a general, that's clear. Even if I wanted to fight a pitched battle with Anchor, I wouldn't do it in town where innocent people would get killed; and, frankly, I've got no interest in just shooting up a lot of men. What I want is to kill their faith in Hansen's leadership, so that they'll quit him and go off to find some easier place to earn their blood money. One more good blow ought to do it, and I think—" He hesitated, finding himself curiously reluctant to state the plan that had come into his mind, although he could see no flaw in it. "I think I see the way to go about it, and at the same time give me a chance to get to Miss Vail and make sure she's all right." He picked up a stick and drew a rough map in the dust. "Here's the plan. . . ."

19

■ Dinner at Anchor was a stiff and unpleasant meal these days. There had been a time, Judith Wilkison recalled, when it had seemed rather pleasant, if a little silly and ostentatious, to dress up after a day in the open and join the family in the candle-lit dining-room. Martha had instituted this ritual many years ago, saying primly that riding-clothes and the smell of horses had no place at the table of civilized people. Martha had also used dinner as a class in manners and decorum, not only for her younger sister but for her father as well; yet in retrospect these evening meals of the past seemed warm and friendly to the girl who now sat in silence, eating mechanically, aware of the old man in his wheelchair at the head of the table, and of the dark-haired girl facing him, and of the empty chair that looked at her across the silver candelabra. It was strange, she thought, how the man's absence could be even more oppressive than his arrogant presence.

Lew Wilkison broke the silence abruptly. "You know, I'd like to see that boy again."

Judith glanced at him. "Who, Dad?"

"Why, that young redheaded fellow. I don't like to make that bad a mistake about a man; but, hell, he looked harmless enough——"

"Dad!" Martha said. She objected to rough language anywhere, but particularly at the table.

Judith glanced at her sister appraisingly; she looked beautiful enough to make the familiar jealousy rise sharply into the younger girl's throat, but the candlelight could not mask the lines of strain about her mouth. Judith felt a small twinge of sympathy, edged with faint contempt: *She's bitten off more than she can swallow. Her ambition was bigger than either her nerve or her stomach; she'd like to back out now, but she can't. Poor Martha.* The dark-haired girl at the foot of the table said, "I don't see how you can talk about him so tolerantly, Dad. He's nothing but a——a sneaking murderer. To shoot down a lot of men in cold blood like that——"

Lew Wilkison said, "Honey, I don't think we'd better talk about sneaking murderers, after the company we've been keeping of late. Personally, any time I wanted a man dead——and it's happened a couple of times——I saw to the job myself, and the fellow was facing me when he died. I'm not criticizing your man, understand; maybe he knows what he's doing. He claims to. I'm still waiting to see the

results. So far all I've seen is bandages and buryings."
Martha was silent, flushing, and the old man went on idly:
"Anyway, I'd sure like to take another look at that boy.
We should have paid his price and bought him out, that's
for certain, but damn if I—excuse me, Martha—I certainly never figured he had that much iron in him. A man
who'd let his ranch burn just to set up an ambush, now,
there's a fine, cold-blooded little devil for you! And having
the nerve to split up his crew like that—two of them waiting along the road to shoot up the stragglers! I wish—"

Judith asked, "What, Dad?"

"Ah, never mind," her father said. "A man makes mistakes as he gets old. Waits too long for things and then
sees time getting short ahead and gets in too big a hurry.
. . . What devilment's that man of yours up to tonight?"
he demanded abruptly of his older daughter. "Has he given
up trying to pin them down in the Hills? I told him that
was no good. The dude's cavalry-trained, he's got a couple
of old hands with him, and the Hills folk will help him
out all they can out of spite against Anchor. Nobody's going to catch half a dozen fighting men in that mess of
canyons until they want to be caught; and Cole's apt to
run himself into another deadfall, trying. This riffraff he's
brought onto Anchor's edgy already. A couple more of
them get shot, and the whole lot will saddle up and light
out of here—"

Martha pushed back her chair and rose. Her face was
white. "You sound as if you wanted that to happen! Anybody would think you didn't want us to win, the way you
talk!"

"Us?" the old man asked gently. "Why, honey, I wasn't
aware that I had a part in it any more, or Judy either.
Cole made it quite plain the last time I had some advice
to offer—"

"He was upset, and can you blame him? He didn't
mean— Just because he was a little rude, you don't have
to act as if—as if it was all our doing. Cole's and mine!
Don't forget, you tried exactly the same thing yourself,
twelve years ago; and you certainly didn't do any better
than Cole's doing. At least—" She checked herself, startled

125

at what she had been about to say.

"At least Cole's still got the use of his legs?"

"I'm sorry, Dad. I didn't mean— But it's a little late for you to get high-minded now," she gasped. "After all these years of telling us how the whole Basin was rightfully ours. And as for Cole—" She hesitated, then cried, "As for Cole, you brought him here. You picked him; I didn't!"

"Honey," said the old man gently, "I didn't marry him."

The dark-haired girl looked at him for a moment, then snatched up the skirts of her satin dress and ran from the room. Lew Wilkison watched her go. When the door had closed, a look of pain crossed his face and he struck the table lightly with a clenched fist. "If that tinhorn hurts my girl—!"

Judith rose and moved toward the door. The old man's voice followed her: "Judy."

"What is it, Dad?"

"I didn't mean that like you took it."

She glanced back. "I didn't take it any way. I'd just finished eating, that's all."

"You're my girl, too," Lew Wilkison said. "You know that. Only—she looks like her mother. Your mother."

"I know," Judith said. "You've said that before. I just look like you, worse luck for me."

This was a rough game they often played together, not entirely without malice. The old man chuckled. "You're going to be all right, Sister. I'm not worrying about you."

Judith said, "You never did, to amount to much."

Her father looked at her slyly and said, "If you don't stop growing, you're going to be too tall for the boy. He's a little short for you already, isn't he?" She did not speak and he said, "Do you think I'm blind, Sister?"

"I don't know what you're talking about," she said.

"This redheaded squirt. A big girl like you would have to handle him careful or he'd break."

She drew a long breath, turned, and said calmly, "Cole's been trying to break him without much success."

"Cole hasn't been able to catch up with the boy."

"He's no boy," Judith said. "And he's not so damn small, either."

"You're stuck on him, aren't you?"

"Why, hell, yes," she said. "Why not? He's ten years older than I am, he's going to marry another woman, and I've only spoken to him a couple of times in my life. Besides which, he's probably busy right now trying to figure the best way to ruin the whole Wilkison family. Why shouldn't I be madly in love with him?"

The old man in the wheelchair chuckled again. "Sister, you can take him away from that prissy little town girl without half trying."

Judith said, "Prissy isn't quite the right adjective, Dad, according to reports I've heard. But I'm sure Mr. Parrish knows what he's doing and why, and I certainly wouldn't want to enter into competition——"

Her father made a rude noise. "Why the hell not? If you want the man, take him. Don't sit around the house moping. *She's* not going into the Hills after him, is she? Why, she'd faint if she found herself out of sight of a house or road. Go out there and find him, Sister. Tell him I'll pay his price for his ranch, and five thousand more, call it dowry. All he has to do is take you out of the Basin. . . . What's the matter now? What did I say wrong?"

She licked her lips. "That's quite a bonus, Dad. Five thousand dollars and me, just so Martha and her husband can live in peace!" She turned away.

His voice checked her at the door. "Judy!"

She said without looking back, "What is it now?"

"You don't give the old man credit for much, do you? It could be I'm just trying to get you out of this mess I've made here, couldn't it?"

"It could be," she said stiffly. "I'll work on trying to believe it."

"I have tried to be fair," her father's voice said. "If I have favored your sister a little, it's something I can't help, for which I try to make amends. In material things I have treated you alike, haven't I? Half the ranch will come to you when I die; Cole and Martha both know that. And what I was trying to say a little while ago—I put it poorly, I know—was that I'd like to see you safely away from

here with a man of your own choosing; and that if it's regard for my feelings that's holding you back, because he's
fighting against us, pay it no heed. I'm too old, Sister, to
hate a man merely because he stands against me, which
does not mean I won't smash him when I get the chance."

"Dad," she said, "Dad, I—"

"You've never waited for my permission to do anything
you wanted," the old man went on. "But if it's my permission you need, you have it. Take the fellow away from
here before he breaks your heart by getting himself killed.
The odds are too heavy against him. I make fun of Cole,
but the man is cold and ruthless, and he's going to win. In
the long run, Sister, it's weight that counts, weight and
power. A small man with brains and guts can make a
fight of it, but in the showdown the stronger man always
wins, and there's always a showdown, sooner or later. If
you want him, you'd better get to him while he's still alive.
A dead man's no use to anybody."

She looked at him for a moment and started to speak;
but there was nothing to say, and she turned abruptly and
ran out of the room and upstairs to her own bedroom,
where she threw herself on the bed, gripping the covers
tightly. Presently she drew a long breath, sat up and
straightened her hair, and rose and looked at herself in the
full-length wall mirror. She grimaced at the sunburned girl
in the fussy silk dress who looked back at her.

You look too healthy to be human, she told herself
grimly. *What you need is about three weeks in a dark
cellar*.

She had begun to unfasten the dress impatiently, when
she became aware of her sister standing just inside the
door, watching her. Martha studied her for a moment, and
took the key from the lock.

"Dad's an old fool. You're not going anywhere tonight,
Miss."

Judith said, "One of these days you're going to lose an
ear, listening at keyholes." After a moment, she added,
mildly, "Dad's romantic. I wasn't going anywhere."

"Then why are you changing clothes?"

"Maybe because I don't like looking like a dressed-up

128

horse. One of these days I'm going to start picking my own clothes, instead of wearing what you think is suitable and ladylike. I certainly couldn't do worse than this!" After a moment, Judith glanced at her sister curiously. "Why mustn't I go anywhere *tonight*, Martha? You sound almost as if it would be all right if I planned to go tomorrow night."

The older girl smiled in a way that briefly made her mouth look almost ugly. "Tomorrow night will be perfectly all right, dear. But you'll be wasting your time." The smile vanished and she cried abruptly, "How could you do such a thing, you, a Wilkison? Does everything Dad and I have done for you mean nothing at all to you? Why, even now—even now I'm protecting you from the consequences of your own heedless actions. Cole doesn't know. If he did, I'd hate to think—"

"Martha, what the hell are you talking about?" Judith demanded, bewildered.

"That's right, swear at me!" the dark-haired girl cried. "I've done my best. I've tried to make a nice home here for you and Dad, the kind of home people of our standing ought to have. I've tried to—to do what's best for Anchor and the family, even when it wasn't—wasn't pleasant. In our position, we have a certain responsibility, both to ourselves and to other people who look to us for leadership. Next year, or the year after that, this territory is going to become a state, and its affairs are going to be run by—by men with vision and ambition, not old fogies like Dad who are satisfied to run a few cattle and squabble endlessly with their neighbors and talk about what they might have done if luck hadn't been against them. Luck! If he'd used a little sense, he wouldn't have got himself shot up—"

Judith said sharply, "It doesn't seem to me your man's doing much better!"

Martha stared at her. "*You* have the insolence to say that? After what you did? At least Dad only had himself and his recklessness to blame; he wasn't betrayed by his own family! Do you think we don't know that you rode over to Rafter H that day—"

Judith started. "I see. That's how Dad learned. . . .

But I didn't betray anybody," she said quickly. "I was trying to prevent a murder, but I went to the wrong place. I did not know of any plans for that night, and I certainly didn't discuss them with Mr. Parrish, Martha."

"Do you think I can believe that? If nobody told him, how did he happen to be waiting at the right time in just that place?"

"Because he has a few brains and had paid some attention to the shape of the country," the younger girl said. "Besides, he wasn't waiting in the one place, he was waiting in two; and as for the time, he'd probably have waited a week, being a patient man, until Cole walked into the trap. I wouldn't want to answer for what I might have done if I'd had knowledge of what Cole was planning, but there was no betrayal that night, Martha."

"You're lying!"

Judith said, "Don't call me a liar, just because your ambition has got you married to a man you can hardly stand to look at, so that you can't bear the thought that he might not have the ability to do what you married him for." She caught her sister's wrist, avoiding the blow aimed at her face. "Don't!" she protested, ashamed and embarrassed for both of them. "Martha, don't. . . . Damn it, don't be a fool!" she cried, suddenly becoming angry as they struggled. "I can wring you out and hang you up to dry, and you've slapped my face for the last time. Now behave, damn it!" She pinned the older girl into the angle between the dresser and the wall. "While we're about it," she panted, "I'll take my key."

Martha opened her hand and let the key fall to the floor. "It won't do you any good!" she gasped. "It's too late; you can't save him this time. By the time you get to town—" She checked herself abruptly, her eyes finding the clock on the dresser, that read no more than eight-thirty.

Judith saw the look, and stepped back, snatching up the fallen key. "Town?" she said softly. "How would Cole lure him into town? He isn't fool enough—"

"Isn't he?" Martha asked. "Not for that little blond creature whose father owns the drygoods store? He's fool

130

enough to want to marry her, isn't he? Oh, he'll come, and that'll be the end of him; and then maybe you'll come to your senses."

Judith turned sharply away from her and kicked the door closed and locked it, palming the key. She was aware of her sister watching her as she pulled off her dress and petticoats hastily and found other garments in the closet; she dressed in a breathless hurry, stepping into her boots as she buttoned her shirt. She started for the door, turned back and snatched a holstered revolver from a hook inside the closet, and ran across the room. Martha stepped close to her as she unlocked the door.

"You can't do it!" the older girl cried. "Why, Cole will —will do something dreadful to me if he learns I let slip—"

Judith said, "You deal with your man, Martha; that's your problem. I'm going to lock you up in here. You can yell, or you can try climbing out the window—although I wouldn't advise it in that dress—or you can wait in dignified silence until Phil Bennett comes by with the key. I'll leave it with him. Don't yell unless you want to get somebody killed." She buckled the gun about her and glanced at the older girl. "It was your idea, wasn't it?"

Martha shook her head. "No."

"I say yes," Judith contradicted. "I know Cole's opinion of women. He wouldn't think any man would be silly enough to risk his life for one."

Martha flushed. "It was still no idea of mine! And you're surely not considering going into town like that!" There was horror in her voice. "In trousers!"

Judith looked up quickly and stared at her sister; she gave a little laugh that was almost a sob, closed the door, and locked it. Then she was running down the stairs and out of the house, around it, and down the gentle slope behind it toward the barn and stables. Men watched her from the bunkhouse door; she was aware of their eyes and of their sly comments, and ignored them, although once no such looks or remarks would have been tolerated on Anchor. The stable floor was dirty underfoot; nothing was kept up these days the way it had been. It was apparently

131

beneath the dignity of men drawing fighting pay to do any work around the place; or perhaps it was, she reflected grimly, simply beyond their ability to do anything more exacting or strenuous than pulling a trigger.

She brought up short, seeing Phil Bennett coming toward her, leading her chestnut gelding, saddled. "Your dad thought you might be riding tonight," the sandy-haired rider said.

She took the bridle from his hand, and stroked the animal's nose briefly, since the caress was expected. "I don't like to be spied upon, Phil," she said without looking around.

"What do you mean, Miss Judy?"

"You told Dad about my going to Rafter H. It had to be you; any of the other men would have told Cole, not Dad."

"Your dad's tied to that chair, Miss Judy. Somebody's got to act as his eyes and ears."

"And mouth," Judith said dryly. "Next time you make your report, damn it, wait till Martha's out of earshot. . . . Here," she said, tossing the key toward him. "Give me five minutes start and let her out. She's locked in my room. Watch out when you open the door; she'll be looking for someone to claw."

"Now, Miss Judy, that's no way to talk about your sister."

She sighed. "No, Phil," she said. "You're right; it isn't. I wish— Tell her I'm sorry."

The moon was not yet up as she rode away, but the night had a curious stillness that made it seem later than it was. She took the road, holding her mount in to save its strength for the ten miles that lay ahead; there was in her mind nothing now but the problem of getting to town in the shortest time possible. What she would do when she got there was something that could be decided later; and how she was going to explain her actions, if successful, to a man who had told her to stay on her own side of the fence was another problem that could wait.

It was not until she reached the last rise in the road from which the ranch could be seen that she looked back, her attention drawn by a curious light, of which she had been aware for a while without realizing it. Now she pulled up sharply, seeing the torchlight glare of the burning barn, that threw the house and the trees around it into sharp silhouette. Curiously, her first reaction was a swift anger at somebody's incredible carelessness. Then guns began to go off back there at rapid intervals, sounding like popcorn in a skillet. Even then she did not grasp what was happening, and the thought of Indians flashed into her mind, although it had been years since the last war-party scare in the neighborhood.

Then she remembered a man's voice saying to her father, "There's nothing you can do on my range that I can't do on yours," and to her, "My sympathy won't prevent me from pulling your home down about your ears, should Cole Hansen give me cause." . . . She found that she had instinctively slid from the saddle and found shelter in a shallow ravine, without taking her eyes from the distant scene of violence. It gave her the helpless feeling of being in a nightmare, and abruptly she turned away, pressing her forehead against the hard, smooth leather of her saddle.

"He didn't have to do that!" she whispered aloud. "If he cared at all, he could have found some other way!"

Presently the firing died away. She heard some horsemen go by on the road above, in a tearing hurry; that would be some of the hands, escaping to warn Cole Hansen in town. She did not call out to them, nor did she move from her hiding place for a long time. There seemed to be no place left for her to go.

20

■ At night, the sprawling little town of Logasa had a more decorative and orderly look than in the daytime, with yellow lamplight illuminating the windows of the houses. From where he lay on the ridge above the town, Parrish could distinguish the dark space made by the street on which Caroline and her parents lived. The faint evening breeze brought him snatches of conversation from the nearest porches; somewhere a woman called for a boy named Jackie, a dog barked, a door slammed. There was a murmur of hoofs and wheels from Hill Street.

Lying there, Parrish could also look back along the ridge and see the little hollow to which he had come with Caroline one evening, it seemed a long time ago. His mare was standing there now. He found himself thinking that everything you did committed you to something else; there was never any break in this relentless chain. He looked at his watch in the darkness; the dim face told him more than the time, and he looked across the town to the northeast, the direction of Anchor, but there was no sign on the horizon, either of success or failure. There probably would not be, at this distance.

The regret that had been with him all day came back strongly now, mixed with apprehension, and he thought, *I should have told them to be careful. I should have ordered them not to shoot at the house. If anything should happen. . . .* But you could not give men orders like that, that might cost them their lives. You had to fight from one side of the fence or the other. He remembered saying as much, not long ago.

He let half an hour pass before he began to work his way down the ridge with extreme caution. There was little cover, and the night was clear. He made slow progress. Presently, crouched behind a clump of brush some fifty yards from the edge of town, he saw a man shift position by the corner of the nearest house. A rifle barrel gleamed dully for an instant; then the man was still again, invisible in the shadows. Parrish flattened himself behind his meager shelter, waiting for the man to move away. He was acutely aware that moonrise would leave him trapped out here, a black shape against the pale earth for anyone to see. Already the sky was lighter in the east.

Yet, in a way, the presence of the Anchor rider was a relief, in that it showed that Hansen was here, something of which Parrish had not been quite certain. The vague and hysterical wording of Caroline's note had left a question in his mind. The message still did not seem like what Cole Hansen would dictate as bait for a trap; apparently the man was capable of greater subtlety than he had hitherto shown. Parrish found himself wondering grimly just what means of persuasion had been used to make Caroline put the message into her handwriting and take it to Dr. Kinsman. A fight like this involved all sorts of innocent people in violence they had not asked for and did not deserve. . . .

He heard the approaching riders even before they entered town; sound carried well on such a still night. Flat on the ground, unmoving, he could follow their progress by ear along Front Street; the steep incline of Hill Street slowed the tired horses to a stumbling trot; then they were running again, pounding up to the Vail house and pulling to a halt at the gate.

A man shouted, "Cole! Hey, Cole, where the hell are you?"

The street, that had seemed deserted a moment before, came briefly alive as the shout awakened the shadows; in every pool of darkness that could hide a man, a figure stirred uneasily. Parrish marked the positions down from where he lay. He could not see the house clearly, but he heard Cole Hansen step out onto the porch and speak to

135

the newcomers in a sharp and warning undertone; he was answered by harsh laughter.

"Tip off who? The damn dude's not coming here tonight; he's got other things on his mind besides calling on his girl."

"What the hell do you mean?" Hansen demanded.

A second man's voice said angrily, "Why don't you wake up, Cole? You're not fighting a white man, you're fighting a goddam Apache. Christ, they had the barn fired before we knew there was anyone around; when they opened up on us they had all the light they needed to shoot by, and all we could see was the muzzle flashes in the damn cottonwoods . . ."

Hansen interrupted with a question, but men were coming out of hiding now, up and down the street, and there was a confused hubbub of voices that drowned out, for Parrish, what was being said. He crouched behind his bush, waiting, watching the corner of the house closest to him; at last the man there stepped out into sight and stood for a moment looking uncertainly up and down the ridge, as if he felt himself under observation. A sharper note to the babble of voices made him look around, and he swung away and moved toward the sound. Parrish gave him time to reach the street, then rose and darted into the unoccupied space. Presently he chanced a look around the corner. Cole Hansen was standing at the Vails' gate in the attitude of a man at bay.

"Fifty men, hell!" he was shouting. "You expect me to believe that? All he's got is five men and a cook, and some of those are shot up." There was a growl of protest from the three newcomers, but Hansen raised his voice, overriding them. "Don't try to tell us you were attacked by an army, just because the bunch of you were asleep or drunk. . . . Well, what were ten of you doing, to let half a dozen—?"

"I tell you, Cole—"

Hansen took a step forward. "And I say you're lying, Chip! I say you three boys cooked up a story between you, but damn if anybody here swallows it! If you'd been surrounded by fifty men, you'd never have managed to break

136

out to get here. What's the matter, has this redheaded squirt got you so scared now you cut and run for it the minute he opens fire?"

There was a pause; then the other man's voice said softly, "I'm not scared of him, or of you either; and no man calls me a liar, particularly a big blowhard who has to hire his shooting done for him—"

The group by the gate split apart hastily, leaving an open lane in which the two men faced each other. Cole Hansen's movement was a curious, two-handed gesture, one hand bringing the revolver out and the other slashing across to strike the hammer. Three shots made a stuttering wave of sound; the gun of the man called Chip never fired at all, but tumbled from the holster as its owner fell.

Presently Hansen spoke very gently, "Anybody else like a try? Pinky? What about you, Holahan? . . . All right, then! Take him down to Gosnell's and pick up your horses; we're riding. I'll be along in a minute."

He stood there for a moment, feeding fresh shells into his weapon; then he wheeled, turning his back to the crew. His back made a broad and inviting target, and more than one man behind him stirred uneasily, watching him walk into the house. The door closed behind him. Watching, Parrish drew a slow breath, and thought, *He can't hold them much longer, even with a gun; the next time they'll kill him and pull out.* Strangely, he felt no triumph; victory was very near, tonight, but it was a cheap and tasteless kind of victory. There was no glory in cleverly and carefully cutting the ground from beneath a man and watching him fall. Parrish seemed to hear a girl's voice saying, "I'm afraid I don't like clever and careful men, Mr. Parrish."

A scream from the house across the street made him start, reaching for his gun. He heard a crash of breaking glass and overturned furniture, and looked desperately around. The men in the street were taking an endless time picking up their fallen companion and loading him onto his tired horse. Now they stopped, listening to the noise from the house; Parrish heard their comments and laughter as he crouched in the shadows, helpless. It was the one

137

thing he had not anticipated; he had expected Hansen either to take Caroline with him or, more likely, to leave her here under guard. This direct, wanton, brutal, and pointless kind of revenge was so foreign to his own nature that he had made no effort to guard against it, although it seemed obvious enough now.

He looked about him for some way of reaching the house without running the gauntlet of the whole Anchor crew; he swore at them softly for tarrying and he cursed his own stupidity in placing himself on this side of the street. And suddenly he knew that the night had gone completely wrong in this moment. You could taste an unsuccessful plan; you could smell it; it had the same taste and odor as a lost battle. Victory was a long way off; and for all his cleverness and carefulness he was standing, at this critical instant, on the wrong side of the street with twenty-odd men between him and the girl he had come to save. He heard a whimpering cry from the house, and he cocked his gun and started forward recklessly, but he drew back as Hansen came into sight alone.

The big man stood on the porch for a moment, pulling on his gloves; abruptly he kicked the door closed behind him so hard that the sound of the breaking hinge was like a shot, and the door rebounded to hang crazily behind him. He walked down the path without looking back and put his foot against the gatepost; he seemed only to lean against it, but the post snapped off, carrying with it the gate and a section of the white fence. Hansen kicked the wreckage out of his way and strode off down the street, followed by his crew, now silent.

Reaching the porch a moment later, Parrish paused for an instant to listen, in case Hansen should have left a man inside. But he could hear only the harsh sound of Caroline's sobbing, which drew him forward past the loosely dangling door into the Vails' living-room, no longer familiar. He looked at the scene with a sense of shock and anger that was mixed with guilt for his own part in bringing this destruction here. Hansen had smashed the room thoroughly, after first placing the lamp safely on the mantel-piece to give himself light to work by. There was not a whole picture on the wall; there was not a piece of furniture that was not damaged. Even the big sofa stood askew, its cushions scattered and one leg broken. Caroline was there; half lying on it, half kneeling beside it, looking very much like a discarded doll.

He hurried forward and knelt beside her. She stirred, choking on a sob, when he reached for her. "Oh, don't!" she gasped. "Don't touch—" Then she looked around quickly, and sat up. *"Johnny!"*

Even in that moment, he noticed, she had time to think of her appearance, pushing the loosened and matted fair hair back from her face with a quick motion.

"Johnny!" she cried. "What are you doing here? I thought you were—they said—"

Her voice trailed off. He was shocked to see fear come into her eyes as she looked at him. She licked her lips, pushing herself a little up and away from him. Some instinct made her at the same time reach down to flick her disordered skirt into place, covering her ankles modestly.

"Johnny, what's the matter, honey?" she whispered. "You don't think— Why, I tried to warn— I declare, you can't blame—"

He watched her, bewildered. There was a bruise on her cheek, and the tears had given her face a puffed and splotchy look; but he had seen her cry before and could overlook and even sympathize with her appearance, under the circumstances. It was the furtive and frightened way she faced him that he did not understand. Then he noticed how she was dressed, in the fashionable blue traveling-suit she had worn to the ranch a few days ago. The costume was in a sadly rumpled state now; Cole Hansen had apparently hooked his big fingers into the front of the jacket, twisting and crushing the cloth as he shook her violently. Yet it seemed an odd way for her to be dressed at this time of night in her own home. She made a quick, almost sly attempt, under Parrish's eyes, to pull her clothing straight, as if its dishevelment were evidence of some nameless guilt.

"Honey," she gasped, "honey, don't look at me like that!"

"Caroline—"

"I tell you, I couldn't help it! He made me write it, he did! He. . . . I declare, honey, you know I'd die rather than do anything to hurt you, but he—he threatened Mother and Dad, and I couldn't. . . . You believe me, don't you?" Suddenly she was clinging to him. "You've got to believe me, Johnny! I didn't mean. . . . We never thought you'd really, I mean, I *did* try to warn—!"

Her small hands gripped him tightly. He heard the movement behind him, but he could not free himself in time to move out of the path of the blow.

21

■ Never quite unconscious, Parrish was aware of Caroline's instinctive withdrawal as he crumpled under the blow. It was a final proof of betrayal, if any was needed: that she should pull disdainfully away from contact with him instead of trying to help and support him. . . . A belated wave of pain ran through him, washing away all conscious thought. He knew he was on the floor, and he knew when someone slipped his gun from the holster. Blackness swirled about him and receded. He could hear them talking above him.

". . . thought you'd never come, honey!" This was Caroline's voice, breathless with relief. "Hadn't you better —tie him up?"

The man's voice had a thick, slurred, unfamiliar sound; it also held an odd note of curiosity. "Doesn't it mean any more than that to you, Caroline?"

"Mean any more than what? Honey, I declare I don't know what you're—"

"He was going to marry you. He came here to save you, thinking you were in trouble."

"Save me!" she cried. "Heavens, a fine job of saving he did! Look at my face, my clothes! Look what that beast did to Mother's living-room, just because of him. Honey, *please* tie him up! And then get the buggy and go after Hansen. Maybe you'd better take a horse; it's faster."

There was a brief pause, then the man laughed. "Hansen? What the devil do you want me to say to Hansen, Caroline?"

"Why, that we've got—him here."

"And what in the world do you expect to gain by that, now?"

She said stiffly, sensing ridicule, "I expect to gain the money, what else? The thousand dollars Hansen promised us."

The words crawled sluggishly through Parrish's brain, making the whole ugly situation at last quite clear. The man standing above him laughed again, on an incredulous note.

"Caroline, Caroline, do you really think Hansen is going to pay us anything, after what's happened?"

"But we've kept our part of the bargain!" Caroline cried shrilly. "I declare, don't you men *ever* keep your promises?"

"Asking him for money right now would be committing suicide, darling. The man's raging mad. He'd still figure we're lucky to be left with our lives, after the way our little plan misfired." The man went on calmly: "Furthermore, I don't think I want to be around Cole Hansen right now. I don't think his prospects are very good. God only knows where Parrish got hold of fifty men, but if that report's correct, you know Hansen's bunch of cutthroats aren't going to stand up to the odds. They're mutinous already."

Caroline's voice was a cry of despair: "But if the Rafter H crew should win—what will they do to us?" She stamped her foot in anger and fear. "It was your idea! The whole thing. And now look. . . . What are we going to do?" she gasped. "Why, we haven't even enough money to pay our fare to the railroad, let alone—" Suddenly she was silent. When she spoke again, it was in a completely different tone, crisp and businesslike: "Tie him up, honey. Keep an eye on him; we may need him to get away from here. If we meet his crew, we'll just give him back to them; no matter how he feels, he won't let them hurt me—"

"What about me, Caroline?" The man's voice was dry and amused. "He might not be so magnanimous about me."

"Ah, he won't let them lay a finger on you, honey. You don't understand Mr. Parrish. Somewhere inside him there's a redheaded temper to go with his hair, but his Dad and the Yank army between them put the poor little thing in handcuffs, and he's never let it out since. Why, I've teased the man within an inch of his life, and he's never acted like anything but a perfect little gentleman. . . . Well, almost never." She went on quickly, amid rustling sounds of movement: "Heavens, I took a fright! I don't suppose I can take time to change. . . . Where do you think my bonnet could have got to in this mess; it was lying right on the table there."

"Caroline, what are you going to do?"

"It's all right, honey. Dad would want me to do it, if he was here. There's enough; I saw it when he closed the safe tonight and I know where he keeps the key."

"I'll have no part in it!" The man's voice had a shaken sound. "I don't want to spend the rest of my life waiting for a policeman to tap me on the shoulder. Your parents will blame me; they dislike me already; they'll have the law—"

Caroline laughed. "Honey, you're being silly. Dad wouldn't go to the law and let everybody know that his own daughter had robbed him; even if he wanted to, Mother would never let him. I tell you, if they were here tonight, and understood the situation, Mother would make him give me the money, even if she doesn't like you." Her voice hardened. "I told you, George Menefee, I'd do anything to get out of this dreadful place, anything; and don't you dare to criticize! I've waited long enough for you to do something; all I have to show for your cleverness is a

142

black eye and a ruined dress. Now I'm going to do it my way, honey. You just keep an eye on him and don't let him get away, hear?"

Parrish heard her footsteps and the whisper of her skirts go away from him. Presently the room was quiet; outside, there were sounds of movement in the neighboring houses, but no one had yet mustered up courage to investigate what had happened here. The townspeople had long since learned that it was better not to meddle in Anchor business. Parrish did not move, or open his eyes, even when a toe nudged him sharply in the ribs.

"You can sit up now, John." The nudge was followed by a deliberate kick. "Damn you, don't play possum on me!"

After a moment, Parrish sat up; the effort started a dizzy pounding in his head. He looked up at George Menefee as his vision cleared, and understood the reason for the indistinct sound of the man's voice. One whole side of the lawyer's pale and normally handsome face was swollen and discolored as the result of, apparently, one tremendous blow of Cole Hansen's fist. In other respects, Menefee had the same dusty, disheveled, and roughed-up look that Caroline had displayed: he had ripped one knee of his trousers somehow, perhaps in falling. In his right hand he held Parrish's revolver, cocked; in his left, the short stove poker he had used to strike with, earlier.

"Well, I've got to hand it to you, John," he said softly. "You turned the tables on all of us, very neatly. It's a pity you had to spoil it for yourself by coming here at all; but I knew you would. I tried to tell Hansen to wait, that you'd still show up, but he wouldn't listen, the stupid ox!" Menefee tossed the poker aside and touched the side of his face gingerly; then he smiled. "But I was right. I knew that note would bring you, and it did. There's nothing quite as chivalrous as a good, upright citizen with a guilty conscience, is there, John?" He chuckled. "Ah, don't blush. Caroline has no secrets from me."

Parrish whispered, "Now there's a pleasant thought for a man to entertain about a woman!"

The other man's smile did not waver. "She was always

143

mine, John," he said softly. "Always. Make no mistake about it. You were never a man to her; you were only transportation East. She and that mother of hers have been watching the stage for years, looking for likely young men coming to town; sick as you were, with money in your pocket, you were a perfect prospect. It was interesting to watch, since I'd had the technique used on me a year or two earlier. However, the difference was that I knew within two minutes of our first meeting what kind of a girl she was, what she wanted, and how far she was willing to go to get it. We understood each other perfectly. If it hadn't been for my congenital inability to read a poker hand correctly, and the crooked dealers down at Morgan's . . ."

There was something indecent about this delving into the debris of shattered human relationships, and Parrish looked away, glancing about the wrecked room as Menefee talked on. Finally he brought his attention back to the lawyer, noting the man's taut posture and the wary and inexpert way he held the big revolver. It occurred to Parrish that the other man was afraid of him; but there was something more than fear in the lawyer's voice. There was also hatred behind the effort at lightness, and Parrish knew a sudden twinge of apprehension as he understood that Menefee was talking to convince himself.

"If it hadn't been for the money," Menefee said, "she'd never have left me. The money, and the hope that you would take her East, as I had proved unable to do. But the minute you no longer offered her that hope, she came back to me. Are you wondering why I took her back, knowing—knowing what you had been to each other?" The lawyer licked his lips, no longer smiling. "Of course I took her back. You see, I happen to love her. No, not the pretty, dainty, sweet notion of her that you were planning to marry; what would a man like me do with a girl like that? Caroline and I understand each other, up to a point. I'm afraid she tends to underestimate me a little, however, or she would never have left me here alone with you, John." Suddenly the revolver lifted and steadied. "I'm afraid I'm going to have to kill you, John."

Parrish looked up into the bore of the weapon, able to see the lands and grooves of the rifling. "Why?" he asked softly.

"You need to ask why? Three years of watching her making up to you, throwing herself at you, cheapening herself for a man who considered himself too good—"

"That's not true."

"You were willing enough to take what she offered, but what did you give in return? I failed her, true, but at least I loved her and still do. If it hadn't been for you—"

"If it hadn't been for me," Parrish murmured, "it would have been someone else, George."

The man above him smiled. "Ah, I'm glad you said that. You make it very easy for me. Not that it would have been difficult in any case. I've had a long time to hate you, my friend; whatever happens afterward, this night is not a failure if it sees you dead."

Parrish said quietly, "It's a single-action gun, George. You'd better cock it first."

It would not have worked with a more experienced man, but Menefee was but poorly acquainted with firearms, and aware of his own deficiency. His glance dropped uncertainly to the already drawn-back hammer of the revolver, and Parrish lunged, striking the weapon up as he rolled in under the barrel. The gun discharged over his head; then he had cut the lawyer's legs from under him and Menefee crashed backward to the floor. Parrish was on top of him, finding his gun arm and beating it club-like against the leg of an overturned chair. Menefee cried out at the pain and opened his fingers, and the weapon spun away from him. Parrish had it and was on his feet before the larger man could rise.

They were both breathing heavily. Parrish felt the steady pulse of pain in his head; it made his voice harsher than he had intended. "You shouldn't have tried to play this game with me. It's my game. I wouldn't attempt to fight you in court. Stick to the law, George. . . . No, you're fine where you are; don't get up." He cocked the revolver. "I said, don't get up!"

Menefee got to one knee. His collar had come unfastened in the struggle and his waist coat was awry; the expression of his face was a ghastly caricature of his usual mocking smile. "Shoot, you fool," he gasped. "Don't you know you're going to have to kill me?"

For the second time that night, Parrish had the helpless feeling of watching a situation slip out of his control. Menefee rose deliberately to his feet and started forward. There was all the time in the world; Parrish could have killed the lawyer five times as he advanced, or shot his legs from under him. Yet there was something here that would not let him shoot; there was suddenly too much between them to be erased by a few ounces pressure on a trigger.

Parrish heard himself laugh. "Why George," he said, "I doubt that you can make me do anything you say, even kill you." He lowered the hammer of the gun expertly and tossed the weapon behind the sofa. "But you are welcome to try," he said.

As he stepped forward, he felt suddenly light and free. It was a damn-fool thing to do; and it was, he knew, something he had wanted to do for a long time. There were times a man had to act like a damn fool, for the good of his soul.

22

■ He did not wait for Menefee to reach him. Cold logic said that, as the smaller man, it was to his advantage to stay out of close quarters where the lawyer could bring his weight to bear; but instinct told him to carry the fight to Menefee. This cluttered room was no place for strategy anyway, nor was he in a mood for it; there had been enough strategy for one night. He moved in fast, under the left hand the lawyer threw at him, took a glancing right on the cheekbone, and, in close, hammered hard at Menefee's belt, feeling the softness there, before the lawyer tied him up. As the larger man's arms closed about him, Parrish threw himself back and down, carrying his adversary down on top of him. He drew up his knees as he fell, catching Menefee's full weight upon them. The shock broke the lawyer's embrace, but Parrish's injured head hit the floor hard, dizzying him.

They rolled apart. Parrish, trying hazily to rise, was aware of Menefee catching his breath, scrambling up, and snatching up a broken chair to strike with. *Your mistake, George*, Parrish thought, *you should have stuck to fists; clubs and guns aren't your style*. He waited out the blow, unmoving, and rolled inside it as the last moment, clutching the lawyer's legs and bringing him down again. They came to their feet together this time. Parrish took a stinging right to the side of the head, moving in; it made the room go hazy again, and he leaned against Menefee for support as he pounded the softness of the belt line with both hands and felt the taller man give way a step under the beating. It was the first break of the fight, and it told Parrish that his instinct had been correct. This was a man who would box you all day, but who could not stand up to a real pounding.

Menefee seized him and tried with his knee. Twisting, Parrish avoided the blow, drove his hands up, and closed his fingers about the larger man's throat; furniture splintered as they fell together. Menefee rolled, chopping at Parrish's head and shoulders in a panicky way; then he clawed at the hands throttling him, caught a finger, and started bending it backward. Parrish released his grip and rolled free. Rising, he tripped over the disordered rug; Menefee was on top of him before he could regain his balance, driving him down and beating his head against the floor, so that a sick blackness swirled about him. It was a wide-open fight now and he used his knee without compunction; he missed, but Menefee's quick sideways movement gave him a chance to break free and roll clear. When he tried to rise, he was startled to find that he could not make it. The room was swaying about him and he could not see clearly.

He crouched there on hands and knees. A little distance away, Menefee rose, looked about him, and found the chair he had used before. He swung it up. Parrish saw it coming and managed to sway out of the full path of it; it broke against his shoulder and knocked him over. Menefee kicked him hard in the ribs and swung the remnants of the chair a second time. It was a poor weapon now and the glancing blow, as Parrish twisted aside, did little damage. He caught the lawyer about the legs. Menefee tried to kick himself free, but tripped on the rug and fell.

Parrish scrambled to his feet, swaying. Nothing was very clear in his mind, and the taste of blood and anger was in his mouth. He watched Menefee rise, and moved in. The lawyer side-stepped his charge and knocked him down. Parrish rose. Menefee's laugh reached him dimly as he moved in again. Confident now, Menefee awaited him and knocked him down again. Parrish shook his head to clear it, rising a third time, seeing the lawyer awaiting him, battered but triumphant. *You crow too soon, my friend,* Parrish thought. He took a blow in the face and a stiff low right to the body that should have hurt but did not; then he had his chin against the taller man's shoulder as he pounded hard against the vulnerable belt line and felt Menefee yield and move back. There was a grim rhythm to this fight; they had been through this sequence before. The lawyer grappled with him, but his hands did not have the strength of previous occasions, and Parrish arched his back against the embrace and continued to hammer at Menefee's midsection, driving Menefee back step by step until he reached a wall and could go no farther.

"Enough!" The lawyer's arms dropped. His voice was a gasp, forced out of him by a blow. "Enough!" he breathed.

Parrish stared at him, uncomprehendingly. His own breath whistled shrilly between his teeth and a red fighting haze seemed to hang between him and the other man. "George, you're a fool," he panted, and took the lawyer by the throat, vaguely annoyed at the stupidity of a man who would start a fight like this and think it could be ended by a word, like a boy's squabble. He watched the panic that came to Menefee's eyes become dulled with the film of approaching unconsciousness; slowly the man went slack beneath his hands and slid to the floor.

"That's enough," a voice said behind him. "You're killing him."

There was something odd about the presence of the voice in this place at this time, but he had no strength to waste upon the problem. "Yes," he said.

"Let him breathe," the voice said.

"No."

"Damn it, let him go or I'll bend this gun barrel over your head!"

Parrish looked around. Judith Wilkison stood there, slender and inexplicable in the yellow lamplight. Her expression was no help to him, but the raised revolver in her hand carried authority. He opened his hands and stood up; this was a mistake, causing the room to reel about him. He stumbled to the wrecked sofa and sat down, burying his face in his hands. It seemed as if he would never get enough air to breathe, nor did the surging pain in his head diminish appreciably; but gradually the madness of the fight drained out of him, leaving him sick and empty. He watched the tall girl in boy's clothing kneel by the unconscious man on the floor. Presently the lawyer opened his eyes and sat up weakly.

Parrish said, "I was wrong, George. It seems that you can make me want to kill you, after all."

Menefee licked his lips, looked from Parrish to Judith Wilkison, and said nothing. The girl stood up. She started to put her gun away, but checked herself and glanced at Parrish's empty holster.

Parrish said, "It's behind the sofa, Miss Wilkison."

"I know." She glanced at him, frowning faintly. "But why do you tell me?"

"Perhaps I would rather you had it than he."

She said quietly, "That may be an error in judgment on your part, Mr. Parrish. I—" She checked herself abruptly, listening. The high, clear notes of Caroline's voice, speaking to someone outside, came through the front door.

Judith stepped quickly around the sofa and picked up Parrish's discarded weapon; she moved to the door, standing flat to the wall beside it.

". . . yes, I'm all right, thank you, Mrs. Boylan," Caroline was saying. "Yes, we had a little trouble, but it's all right now. . . . No, the folks aren't home; they went visiting over to the Lawrences' for the evening. . . . Why shouldn't I go inside?" The other woman's words were indistinct. Caroline said, "A fight? Well, I declare, I'd better go see. . . . Men are so silly, aren't they, Mrs. Boylan, always fighting about something." She came running up the path and stopped on the porch. "George! George! Is everything all right, honey?"

By the door, Judith Wilkison drew the hammer of Parrish's revolver to cock and aimed the weapon across the room at George Menefee. The lawyer looked at her, hesitated, licked his lips again, and spoke.

"Come—come on in, Caroline. Everything's fine."

She came through the door breathlessly, still holding her skirts as she had lifted them to run. Then she let them fall, looking at the room and at the two men who occupied it within her field of vision. Abruptly she giggled, on a note of hysteria.

"I declare, if you two don't look—"

A movement behind her made her start and jerk around, to see Judith Wilkison and the gun she held.

It was the first time that Parrish had see them together. The comparison was not favorable to Caroline; her prettiness was wispy and disheveled tonight, and strain had put a sharpness and a hardness on her features that made the taller girl look the more feminine of the two despite the boy's clothes she was wearing. They faced each other thus for measurable seconds; then Caroline's glance dropped to the gun in Judith's hand and, suddenly scornful, swung from there to the face of George Menefee.

Menefee said, "Caroline, I—" and stopped.

Caroline sighed. Slowly her face changed, becoming soft and at the same time weary. "It's all right, honey," she murmured. "It's all right. I wouldn't have done it for you, either, I reckon. We're not that kind of people, are we?"

She swung back to the girl by the door. "What happens now?"

"To you?" Judith asked. "Why, nothing, as far as I'm concerned. All I want is Mr. Parrish, there. His crew has taken my father and sister into the Hills with them. . . . What's the matter, Mr. Parrish?"

Parrish said, "It was not done by my orders."

Judith's lips were stiff as she said, "A commander is responsible for the conduct of his troops, Captain Parrish."

Parrish said, "I was not making excuses, Miss Wilkison. I was stating a fact."

"Your facts don't interest me," Judith said, and turned back to Caroline. "As far as you're concerned, and that man over there, you can do what you damn well please; but I suggest you do it outside the Basin."

Caroline flushed. "We made a bargain with Anchor," she said, a certain stubbornness in her voice.

"If it's the bargain I think," Judith said, "you made it with my brother-in-law, and you can discuss it with him if you wish, but I wouldn't advise it. Can you ride, Mr. Parrish? I have an extra horse outside that I found up behind the ridge; I think it's yours." She watched Parrish rise and find his hat, and turned again to Caroline. "You probably don't want my advice, but I'll give it to you anyway. Put your man and your luggage in a buggy and head west over Black Mountain Pass right now. You can make it, even in the dark; the stage makes it every other day. If you try to go east across the Basin, you're almost bound to run into somebody with a rope and the desire to use it; or they might find some tar and feathers for you, since you're a woman, and women are generally not hanged around here. You won't like what you find west of the pass, but maybe you can make your way from there, if your man doesn't lose all your money in a mining-camp poker game, as I understand is his habit."

Caroline looked up at the taller girl's face and smiled slowly. "Why, you're just a child," she said. "Honey, I can see through you so plain. I wish you luck, I really do, but always remember that he was mine before he was yours." She turned away, walked across the room to George

Menefee, and sank down beside him, making a pretty and solicitous picture that was by no means unconscious. Judith looked at her for a moment, flushing slightly; then she glanced at Parrish and jerked her head toward the door, looking at him longer than was necessary to convey the message. Parrish moved past her and heard her follow behind him.

23

■ Once he was in the saddle, riding was not as bad as Parrish had expected it to be. The little mare had an easy gait, and he could leave the responsibility for their direction entirely up to the girl who rode beside him, whose prisoner he seemed to be. For the moment he was satisfied with the situation as it stood; his body and mind both seemed to have been drained of strength by the fight, and the events and revelations that had preceded it. He could feel no bitterness toward Caroline Vail; yet neither could he feel any relief at the thought that his obligation to her had been canceled tonight. Human relations could not be added and subtracted as simply as dollars and cents; you could not wipe that kind of a debt off the books at once, even after learning that it had been fraudulently arranged. She had meant something to him once, and even the fact that she had apparently deceived him about her own feelings did not permit him to instantly rearrange his thinking about her.

Judith pulled up. He did likewise and glanced at her in the moonlit darkness, which left her face an enigma in the shadow of her hat. She moved her head curtly. "There's a creek. You'll feel better for washing up. Look better, too."

"Thank you," he said, and dismounted painfully. The water, still icy from the remaining snows up in the Big Gun Mountains, stung his face. He rinsed out his mouth, removed the neckerchief he was wearing range-fashion, wet it, and tried by feel to cleanse the cut that Menefee's poker had opened in his scalp. It had bled more than he had realized. He felt the cloth taken from his hand.

"You'll open it again," Judith said. "Be still now."

He crouched by the water's edge, occasionally rinsing out the cloth as she passed it to him. This place was unfamiliar, and he asked, "Where are we?"

"Don't you know?"

"I wasn't paying attention."

"I don't believe that," she said. There was bitterness in her voice. "I think you pay attention even when you're sleeping, if you sleep. Or do you just lie awake nights thinking of new ways to be ruthless and clever?" He did not speak, and she worked for a while in silence, fashioning a bandage from her own neckerchief. At last she said, "I'm surprised that you'd fight with your fists like that, like any stupid cowhand. You must hate him very much, to want to kill him with your bare hands. I—" She hesitated. "I did not think you capable of so much emotion, Mr. Parrish, particularly when it involved a certain risk."

"There was no risk," Parrish said. "You could look at the man and tell that he was bound to crack as soon as he was hurt a little."

"Well, you certainly took your time getting around to hurting him, then, cowboy," she said dryly, "as your face will testify for some days to come. Why did you throw the gun away, when you could have shot him so easily? Wasn't it enough to kill him? Did you have to smash him first?"

"You were watching the whole thing?"

"I saw no reason to interfere," she said stiffly.

Parrish said, "I don't hate George Menefee. As a matter of fact, I got rid of the gun because I didn't want to kill him. Or cripple him. You never know what a bullet is going to do, no matter how carefully you place it."

153

Judith laughed shortly. "Do you expect me to believe that? Damn it, I had to pry you loose from his throat!"

"I know," Parrish said. "I lost my temper. It's something that hasn't happened since I was a boy, Miss Wilkison, and I'm grateful to you for stopping me." After a moment, he added, "It was the one time Dad took a whip to me, to teach me self-control. He was certain I was headed for the gallows."

The girl said, "I can see that your dad might have had some reason for his belief. But damned if I believe that you took on Menefee barehanded just to protect him."

"No," Parrish agreed. "There were some personal differences that could not be settled with firearms. I've never liked him. But I didn't intend to kill him."

Judith said, "I think you were beating him up for what *she* did to you, which seems a little unfair to the poor man." She did not let him speak, but rose, saying, "I think you can get your hat on over that, Mr. Parrish. Be careful; I don't want you to bleed to death before I can trade you back to your crew for Dad and Martha." She paused beside her horse, and her voice was harsher when she spoke again. "And you'd damn well better hope no harm has come to them."

Parrish glanced at her. "I would hope that in any case."

She said, "I wanted him to kill you. I—I could almost kill you myself, if I didn't need you alive. . . . There'll be nothing left by morning," she whispered. "Two chimneys and some hot ashes. Even the trees were burning when I left!" She was silent for a moment, and he did not speak, and she went on: "Setting the wolves on us! Every rustler and brush-jumper out of the San Loos, every dirt-scratching nester. . . . It was my home," she whispered. "I grew up in that house. My mother died there. And I had to lie out and watch them wreak their hatred on it, smashing and looting, before they set it on fire." Her voice trailed off. At last she spoke in a different tone. "Oh, damn you! Why—?" She left the question unfinished and said curtly, "Well, let's ride. Can you get back into that saddle all right, or do I have to help you with that, too?"

The lopsided moon, not quite a sickle yet, had moved

154

into the western portion of the sky, but was still high over-head, when they stopped again, hearing the sound of distant gunfire. Parrish checked his horse, and the girl stopped beside him. They listened for a while. The sound, coming from the direction of the San Luis Hills to the east, seemed to be moving away from them.

"A bunch of riders chasing somebody," Parrish said softly. "Where are we now?"

"On Anchor," the girl said. "North of the main road. Our road's just over the rise there."

"Why did you bring me here?"

"Because Cole may have learned that you did go to town after all, in which case he'll have sent men to cut you off. He'd expect you to head south from Logasa, since you have friends among the nesters. South and west, to join up with your crew in the San Loos. He wouldn't expect you to ride across Anchor tonight." After a pause, she said, "I couldn't protect you, if his men caught you."

He glanced at her. "Would you want to?"

"Cole would kill you," she said, "regardless of what happens to Martha and Dad. I'm more interested in them, Mr. Parrish; what happens to you is immaterial."

"I—" He checked himself and listened, hearing the desultory popping of distant guns to the southeast. "That's another bunch," he said. "Chasing somebody else."

"Cole's riders will be firing at anything that moves, to-night."

Parrish said, "There's not supposed to be anybody moving on Anchor now. My men are all back in the Hills by this time."

"Do you also give orders to the antelope and jack-rabbits?" the girl asked dryly.

Parrish listened a moment longer and said, "A startled man can fire once at a jackrabbit; he's not going to empty his gun at the beast, Miss Wilkison, nor is the rabbit going to shoot back."

She sighed. "All right, cowboy. I guess you can tell more about shooting than I can; no doubt you've had more practice. All that noise says to me is that we'd better swing wide to the north before trying to reach the Hills. I'm assuming that you want to get back to your outfit as badly as I want to get you there, since I don't really know where to find them. All I know is the general direction they took, leaving the ranch. But you must have arranged a rendezvous with them somewhere." She waited for a response, did not get it, and kicked the chestnut gelding into motion, pulling up sharply when he did not follow. "Come on, Mr. Parrish. We're wasting time. . . . What's the matter?"

Parrish did not speak. He was watching the dark ridge to the east, waiting for a movement he had seen to be repeated. Slowly his hand moved down to his holster, found it empty, and reached for the scabbarded carbine instead, that the girl had not taken from him.

"Careful!"

He looked aside, to see Judith Wilkison aiming his own revolver at him. He said, "Don't be silly, Miss Wilkison. I'm no good to you full of bullet holes."

He pulled the carbine free and touched the mare with his spurs, hearing the girl following close after him. They plunged down into a brushy ravine and climbed out of it; only as he neared the crest of the ridge did Parrish make out the shape of the black horse standing there, occasionally moving a few steps uneasily and then coming to a halt again. The animal was saddled, but there seemed to be no rider around. Parrish pulled up some distance away, dismounted stiffly, and made his approach cautiously on foot. The horse stood watching him come, nervous and uncertain, yet ready to greet the approaching man as a friend.

"There, boy," Parrish said softly. "There, boy, take it easy." He had the dangling bridle now. The black tossed its head but stood still and allowed Parrish to stroke it and talk to it soothingly. "What's the matter, big fellow?" Then he saw the thing that trailed brokenly from the near stirrup. He said sharply, "Stay back, Miss Wilkison."

She was beside him, and said with equal sharpness, "Damn it, cowboy, don't start trying to protect *me*. I've seen deader men than that, some of them your doing." After a moment she added wryly, "But I'll let you see who it is. Here, I'll keep him still."

Parrish put the reins into her outstretched hand and

moved forward. He freed the boot from the stirrup in which it was trapped and turned the body over; but the man had been dragged too far to be recognizable. Parrish found a slicker behind the saddle and spread it over the motionless form.

"Dead?" Judith asked.

He turned on her. "Would he want to live like that? Yes, he's dead. He was shot before he fell; there's blood on the saddle."

"Who is it?"

"I don't know." Parrish pushed at the black horse to turn it so that the brand faced the moonlight. "Lazy T. I never heard of it." There was relief in his voice.

Judith said, "Don't you know your own men, Mr. Parrish?"

He swung to look at her. "My own— What do you mean?"

"Lazy T is a little spread back in the Hills, run by a man named Tate. Two-finger Tate, I think he's called. The story I heard is that some miner didn't like his way of dealing cards and chopped off most of his hand with a Bowie knife when he reached for a pot too hastily. Since then he's been living off other people's beef, mostly Anchor's."

Parrish looked at her for a moment, then bent down and lifted the slicker. After a moment he straightened up, smoothing the covering back into place.

"We'll take the horse along," he said quietly. "Mine has traveled a long way today, and so has yours, by the looks of him." He took the reins from her hand and swung into the dead man's saddle. "Incidentally, it's Tate all right," he said. "I didn't remember; there were quite a few of them that rode into camp this afternoon."

"Where are you going?"

He looked down at her. "Miss Wilkison, were you in a position to learn how many of my men were hit in the attack on the ranch?"

She said, "None of them were hit. I heard them talking. There was only one casualty in the whole fight. Those high-priced fighting men of Cole's apparently folded at the first

157

volley out of the cottonwoods, those that didn't run for their horses and hightail it to town."

"That's what I thought, what I hoped would happen," Parrish said. "But in that case, how did this man get here? I have to find that out, Miss Wilkison. Something's happened here that I don't understand."

He sent the big horse off to the east, shoving his carbine into the dead man's scabbard, which was empty—another indication that he did not like. They mounted the ridge and descended the other side recklessly. The road to Anchor lay below, a pale ribbon in the moonlight. A riderless horse was moving along it aimlessly, limping badly. It shied away as Parrish rode up and cantered in a three-legged fashion out across the range, but not before he had read the Rafter H brand on its hip.

He sat there for a moment, hearing Judith Wilkison come down the road behind him, leading the little white-footed mare. There was a dry taste of fear in his mouth, and his head ached blindingly. Abruptly he spurred the black forward in the direction from which the wounded horse had come. He did not have to go far; just around the curve ahead a dead horse lay in the road, its rider dead beside it. He jerked his mount to a halt and looked down into the empty face of one of his own men, Harry Germack. Judith Wilkison pulled up beside him.

He said, without looking at her, "Will you get him off the road and cover him, while I look around?"

He did not wait for her answer, but sent the big horse up the slope toward something that glinted in the moonlight: a little scattering of empty cartridge cases. Here, behind this rock, a man had made a stand. The rifle lay there, an old-fashioned single-shot, but its owner was not in the immediate vicinity. Parrish found him a hundred yards away along the slope, a heavy-set man in overalls; he would be one of those brought along by the farmer Hinkleman. The rope that had stopped him as he fled on foot was still about him, and the wound in his face was torn and powder-marked by the muzzle blast of the gun that had killed him, so close had it been.

That's three, Parrish thought. *How many more and*

what were they doing here? I told them distinctly— He did not finish the thought, torn between despair and grief and a kind of helpless rage. Abruptly he pulled the carbine from the scabbard and fired it into the air three times. "Rafter H," he shouted. "Yo, Rafter H!"

His voice was shockingly loud in the night; even the shots, with their impersonal quality, had not seemed so loud. The silence that followed seemed endless, and he was about to rein the big black around when he heard his answer: "Over here, Captain."

The voice was very weak. He rode in the general direction from which it had come. Below him, near the road, he could see Judith Wilkison watching him from beside a covered shape. It occurred to him that the task had hardly been one to assign to a woman; but then, she had protested against being shielded from the sight of death.

He lifted his voice again. "Sing out, man. Where are you?"

"Right here, Captain, and don't make so goddamn much noise. If you've got some water—"

Parrish dismounted, took the canteen from the black's saddle, and approached the bushes on foot. The place did not seem big enough to hide a man, just a few rocks and some straggling brush; he was almost on top of the crevice before he saw it. Into it a man had crawled, pulling leaves and branches over him for cover.

"Who is it?" Parrish asked, bending over.

"DeRosa," the man gasped. "Get me out of here, Captain, but take it easy. The damn slug like to broke me in two. Give me some water, first."

"Not for a belly wound," Parrish said.

"Ah, go to hell. I'm finished anyway. Christ, we played hell tonight, both ways. Not a damn thing left in this valley but smoke and ashes and dead bodies, Captain. The place burned real pretty, looked like a wedding cake with candles. The damn crippled old bastard swore at us as long as he had breath to talk. The girl was mad because she'd got her pretty satin dress dirty and we wouldn't let her get another. Never did find the other girl; she'd gone off somewhere. . . . Captain, don't make me die thirsty. I tell you

I'm done for. Numb halfway up my body now. Never did hurt much. . . . Ah, that's better!"

Parrish watched him drink from the canteen greedily. A movement made him look aside, to see Judith Wilkison standing there. He asked her a question wordlessly and she nodded and together they lifted the wounded man out of the crevice and laid him gently on the hillside. Judith went to the horses and returned with a blanket, which she spread over him.

DeRosa opened his eyes suddenly. "Jim's back in the Hills with Wash and Jackson and Cookie. Got the old man and the girl with him; wouldn't let us string the old bastard up or lay hands on. . . . Said you wouldn't like it. The Box Seven boys took care of the little rat that got Silas Purdue. He's hanging from one of the cottonwoods along the creek right now. . . . I reckon I'd never have made an army officer, eh, Captain. Hansen made a sucker out of me . . . all of us . . . my idea . . ."

"What happened?" Parrish asked as the dying man paused for breath.

"Why, it seemed like a hell of a fine idea at the time," DeRosa said, his teeth showing whitely for a moment in his dark face. "Wipe them out, finish it. Knew Hansen would be coming back hell bent for election, once he heard the news. Waited for him along the road. . . . Only the bastard didn't come by the road. Circled around and took us from the rear."

"I told you—" Parrish checked himself abruptly.

"I know." DeRosa grinned again. "Orders. Hit and run. Don't tangle with them. . . . That's what Jim said, but the others had a score to settle. You forgot that, Captain. My idea, maybe, but I didn't have to beat them over the head with it. Not any. So we came back, here." The man's smile widened. "Got to learn this isn't the damn army, Captain. People out here . . . make own mistakes . . . pay for them . . ."

His voice ceased and he was dead. Parrish looked at him for a moment, bleakly, then closed the eyes and drew the blanket over the face that was still smiling at him mockingly. Even in death DeRosa was not one for respect or discipline.

For the moment Parrish knew a terrible hatred for the dead man, whose recklessness and impatience had caused this disaster; yet the fault was not DeRosa's. He, John Parrish, had known DeRosa's character and the temper of the men he was sending against Anchor; he should have been able to predict that they would not have been satisfied with one success. *If I had been there!* he thought bitterly, but that was precisely the point. He had not been there. He had made the one mistake that was unforgivable in a man who asked others to trust and obey him: he had let personal affairs interfere with the matter at hand. The fact that he had given instructions and they had been disobeyed was irrelevant beside the fact that if he had been present he could have prevented this from happening. Instead he had been ten miles away, meticulously and ridiculously discharging an obligation to a girl who was not worth two minutes of any man's time or a drop of his blood. *Ah, don't try to blame her, either!* he told himself sharply. *You know where the responsibility lies.* He wheeled sharply and came face to face with Judith Wilkison.

"I'm sorry," she murmured.

"I see no reason why you should be," he said.

"Don't snap at me," she said. "And don't be too hard on yourself, cowboy. You could not have stopped them."

It did not occur to him to feel more than a mild surprise that she should know what he had been thinking. "Of course I could have stopped them."

"You're not that good," she said. "There's twelve years of hatred behind this; no man could have controlled it. They wanted a crack at Cole. You couldn't have stopped them from taking it."

Parrish started to speak, and stopped, as they both heard it at the same time: the sound of riders approaching fast from the direction of Anchor. The girl grasped his arm.

"You *would* make all that noise!" she said. "Now we're going to have to ride like hell to—"

A strange, dull feeling of resignation had settled over

Parrish's mind. He picked up the carbine he had put aside.

"You ride," he said. "I'll wait for them here." He glanced at her sharply as she did not move. "If it's your dad and sister you're worrying about, don't. Jim won't harm them, no matter what happens to me. He might try a bluff, to save me, but in a showdown he won't let anything happen to a cripple or a woman in his charge, no matter how he feels about them." She still did not move. He said harshly, "Well? It won't do you any good with your family to be found here; they'd be bound to misinterpret your motives."

She said, "You're a blind damn fool, John Parrish. Even that girl of yours could see more than you do. Now stop trying to act like a damn martyr and come along. I know a place up in the Big Guns where you'll be safe for a while."

He looked at her for a moment. The meaning of what she was saying did not reach him clearly. Suddenly everything happening about him had moved a great distance away, and he seemed to be watching it through a telescope that was not properly focused. He was only vaguely aware of being helped onto his horse. Then they were riding endlessly. He knew when morning came, and he knew when it rained for a while and when the sun came out. Still later he could hear a feminine voice swearing unbecomingly at somebody because the person addressed had neither guts nor backbone nor even the fundamental sense of self-preservation that could be found in any self-respecting coyote.

"Hang on, damn you," the voice was saying furiously, "hang on, or I'll lash you across that damn saddle and pack you in like a side of beef."

He remained silent, being a man who made it a policy never to interfere in other people's arguments.

24

■ Parrish awoke slowly from the deep sleep of utter exhaustion to find himself indoors and alone. These were the first bits of information his senses had for him. He sat up abruptly, as odd scraps of memory returned to him, to discover the incredible soreness of—it seemed—every muscle and ligament in his body. It hurt him to move, it hurt him to breathe; he suspected, from the tenderness of one side of his jaw, that it would have hurt him to talk, had there been anyone to talk to.

There was sunlight outside, and he had an impression of early morning and high altitude; it was quite cold. Taking stock of his surroundings, he saw that he was in a crude, one-room log cabin that, in spite of the fact that the dirt floor had been recently swept, gave a strong impression of age and decay. The roof sagged, and weeds had found their way through the chinks between the logs; the whole small building had the air of a man-made structure that the wilderness had enveloped and was in the process of destroying. It had no window, only a door and a rude fireplace. The only furniture was the built-in bunk at one end, upon which he lay. A collection of evergreen boughs and a worn Indian blanket showed where someone else had made a bed on the floor near by.

Then he heard her coming; bushes rustled by the door and she entered the cabin, set aside the Spencer carbine she was carrying, and turned to look at him.

"Well, it's about time you woke up," she said, and tossed something onto the bunk. "There's your shirt; I washed the blood out of it. It's been hanging up since last night; it should be dry enough."

"Thank you," he said.

They looked at each other warily, as if neither of them was quite certain what their relationship should be now. Parrish discovered that, ridiculously, his Eastern training prevented him from feeling quite at ease in the presence of a girl in masculine attire, although he was aware that local usage often condoned such garb for women, on practical grounds. Judith Wilkison had a fresh, scrubbed look; he guessed that she had come direct from washing herself in the icy water of a mountain stream; the edges of her hair were damp. Her slender, tall, and rather leggy appearance in her boy's clothes, with the revolver at her hip, had no counterpart in the standards of feminine beauty he had been taught to accept; yet he found himself thinking that, properly dressed, with the poise and assurance another year or two would give her, she was going to be a very attractive and desirable woman. He dismissed the thought from his mind; this was neither the place nor the time for such notions.

She said, "Damned if you don't look almost alive, for a change. I was afraid I might have to bury you up here; and it would have been kind of a chore, since there's nothing but granite around."

"Where are we?" he asked.

"Up in the Big Guns," she said. "About twenty miles northwest of Anchor, but we took forty miles to get here. The lake hasn't got a name, as far as I know. I came across it when I was a little girl, just riding around; nobody else knows about it." She turned to kneel by the fireplace, poking the coals into life. "It's an old prospector's cabin, I think. I come up here when I get tired of Martha trying to make a little lady of me."

Parrish said, "The one time I talked to your sister, she mentioned that you had a habit of disappearing at times."

"Did she?" Judith seemed uninterested in her sister's comments. "The horses are picketed in a meadow just below the outlet. I made sure we weren't followed; Cole's men picked us up once in the early morning, but I lost

164

them again without much trouble. I know this country better than any imported gunslingers."

Parrish said, "I'm very grateful—"

She glanced at him over her shoulder. "Don't be a fool, cowboy. Your gratitude is nothing to me, and I doubt that it is very much to you. If you're up to it, I suggest that you stagger down to the lake and do something about that beard. It's not very appetizing to look at. Breakfast in fifteen minutes."

The lake, a hundred yards below the cabin, was a deep blue color, with a barren and rocky shoreline. Above it towered one of the peaks of the Big Gun range, seeming quite close; much closer than Parrish had ever seen a mountain of that size before. He could feel the pull of the altitude on his lungs as he shaved and washed, glancing occasionally toward the clump of scrubby pines in which the cabin was hidden, from which rose a faint breath of smoke, soon dissipated. It was an odd, strained situation, to say the least: to be hiding here some ten thousand feet above sea level with a girl whose home he had destroyed, whose family was undoubtedly doing their level best to find and kill him.

When he returned to the cabin, she had food ready. They ate in silence for a while; then Judith took a folded scrap of paper from her pocket and tossed it into his lap.

"I found this in your shirt," she said. "I was going to throw it away, but then I thought you might be saving it as a keepsake."

He set his tin coffee cup aside and unfolded the paper and read the familiar handwriting upon it: *Honey, please come at once. Something dreadful has happened. I must see you right away. Love, Caroline.* He found that it meant very little to him now. People were what they were and did what they had to do. He wadded the paper up and tossed it into the fire, where it flamed up and burned to ashes in an instant.

"She sold you out," Judith said quietly.

"Yes."

"For money?"

"Yes." After a while, he said, "She hates it here. It's a

notion her mother has given her, I think, but it's very real to her. Nothing means anything to her but getting away. I hope she finds the East all she expected."

Judith said, "She'll never get there. That man of hers won't get past the first faro table beyond the pass."

"Then she'll leave him and go on alone," Parrish said. "She'll get there. I just hope she finds the journey has been worth while."

Judith studied his face for a moment. "Why, you really mean that. You must love her a great deal, Mr. Parrish."

"No," he said. "If I had loved her, I would have taken her where she wanted to go. Perhaps it would have been best all around. I don't seem to have accomplished much by staying, besides getting a number of people killed."

She said, "Don't give yourself too much credit, cowboy. A lot of those would have died anyway. Cole would not have taken the whole Basin without a fight; the people around here aren't made that way. You simply made them do their fighting together instead of separately."

Parrish said, "We could have won, if they had obeyed orders. Hansen was beaten when he rode out of town; he would not have had a dozen men left by morning, if he'd been left alone to ride around foolishly looking for revenge. Instead of which the idiots gave him something to strike at, the success he needed to regain control of his crew!" He made his clenched fist relax. "Well, DeRosa's dead and God knows what's happened to the rest; and it's my fault as much as theirs, for not being there."

"What are you going to do now?"

He glanced at her, a little surprised at the question, and at the discovery that he had no plans. "Why, I don't know, Miss Wilkison. It will bear some thinking."

"Well, you can bear this stuff down to the lake and wash it off while you're about it," she said.

Parrish took the skillet and the tin plates and cups. He stopped at the door to look at her. "What about you?" he asked. "You had better get back to Logasa, hadn't you?"

She smiled wryly. "Hardly," she said. "That chestnut of mine is a pretty distinctive horse, Mr. Parrish; they recognized him yesterday morning. I heard them yelling to each

166

other before we pulled away from them. I don't think I want to face my brother-in-law just now. You'll just have to put up with me for a while longer."

She stopped talking and put a hand warningly on his arm, and they stood for a moment at the door like that, listening. Then the distant sound of metal against rock was repeated, and Judith drew in a sharp little breath. "Damn, I shouldn't have used a fire in the daytime. The smoke—"

"There wasn't enough smoke to worry about," Parrish said. He put down the things he was carrying and reached for his revolver, that had been returned to its holster and hung from a peg in the wall near by. "Whoever's out there wasn't brought here by smoke; he knows where he's going. Let's get outside. This cabin's a trap; you can't see out to shoot—"

A man's voice interrupted him. "Yo, the cabin! Miss Judy, are you all right?"

The girl glanced at Parrish. "Why, it's Phil Bennett!" She raised her voice: "I'm fine, Phil. What the hell are you doing here?"

"Running your dad's errands, like always," the man called back. "Can I come in without getting shot up?"

"Are you alone?"

"Just me and my horse, Miss Judy."

The girl laughed. "Well, leave the horse outside."

A moment later Bennett's lean, sandy-haired shape appeared in the doorway. The Anchor rider straightened up to look at the two younger people facing him. After a moment he set his rifle aside and Parrish did likewise with the carbine he had picked up. Judith stepped forward.

"How's Dad?" she asked. "Where is he?"

"Why, he's in town, Miss Judy," Bennett said. "He's all right."

"And Martha?"

"Your sister's feeling fine, now that she's had a bath and got Mrs. French to lend her a dress. She's hanging on Cole Hansen's arm and making plans for rebuilding the ranch twice as big and three times as purty. . . . I wouldn't worry none about Miss Martha."

Judith was silent. Parrish asked, "How did you find us,

Bennett? Miss Wilkison seemed to think this place was a secret of sorts."

"Why, I've been here before," the rider said. "Seven or eight years ago, I guess it was. The Old Man and Miss Martha go worried about Miss Judy and asked me to trail her quiet-like and see where she went when she disappeared like she was in the habit of doing. I reckon they thought maybe she was meeting some boy, even though she was just a kid at the time. I tracked her up here and found she was just playing Indian, in a manner of speaking. When the Old Man sent me out to find the two of you, this seemed a good place to start looking." Bennett looked from Parrish to the girl. "You're sure you're all right, Miss Judy?"

"Yes, of course. Why?"

"Well, Cole's got the story spread around that you've been abducted by this young fellow here. It seems some of the hands caught a glimpse of the two of you yesterday. Cole says they reported Parrish was riding your chestnut gelding and leading a pony with you tied in the saddle; leastways, you didn't seem to be riding right. Cole's got a thousand-dollar price put on Mr. Parrish's head, and everybody in the Basin's after collecting it. There's some bitterness about the way the fighting turned out, and people always like to have somebody to blame. Mr. Parrish makes a good scapegoat. Like always, everybody's jumping out of their boots in their hurry to get over to the winning side."

Parrish grimaced. "Hansen's starting to use his brains at last, it would seem. That thousand dollars of his is going to be the death of me yet, one way or another." He glanced at the man by the door. "Have you got your eye on it, Bennett?"

The older man shook his head. "If God had meant me to get rich he'd have done something about it before this." He took something from his pocket and turned to Judith. "Speaking of money, your dad wanted me to give you this. There's a couple of hundred in the roll; it'll get you away from here. The Old Man says your best bet is to head south to Colonel Christensen's Wagon Wheel spread. The

Colonel and Mrs. Christensen will look out for you. The Old Man will send you more money as soon as he can manage." Bennett grinned. "The Old Man knows damn well who was riding which horse yesterday morning, from the way the two of you vanished in the canyons. No dude three years in the country could have slipped away like that without help. Maybe Cole's figured the same thing. That being the case, Miss Judy, your dad figures you're better out of the Basin for a while."

The girl nodded slowly. "What about Mr. Parrish?"

Bennett said, "Your dad doesn't give a damn about Mr. Parrish, one way or the other. He says you can shoot the little redheaded bastard or keep him for a pet, as you please; but if you want him to stay alive you'd better get him the hell away from here. Cole would like nothing better than to string him up all legal-like with the rest of his men—"

Parrish took a quick step forward. "String who up?"

Bennett looked at him. "That's right, you wouldn't know about it. Why, that's how the Old Man and Miss Martha got freed. Cole's boys caught one of the bunch that had raided Anchor, some fellow out of the Hills. They worked him over for a while, and he told them the hideout. Cole surrounded the camp and caught what was left of your crew flatfooted. They're all in jail now, except your foreman, who tried to pull a gun. Cole shot him. The rest are going to be tried and hanged in legal fashion. Cole wants to sew this whole thing up now, before somebody talks the governor into declaring martial law in the Basin."

Parrish said, "Jim McCloud is dead?"

"They buried him this morning. It was quite a day for funerals; old Gosnell was doing a rushing business."

Parrish was silent for a moment; he swallowed and said softly, "That would leave three men in jail. Jackson, Wash Breed, and Tony, the cook."

"Seven," Bennett said. "Three of the Hills men and a farmer named Hinkleman. There'll be more, I reckon, by the time the trial comes along. They burned out that fellow Kruger last night; he's one Cole's after. His family's in town; they're watching them, waiting for him to show up."

"When's the trial to be?"

"I heard tomorrow."

Parrish looked at the taller man bleakly. He glanced at the girl, picked up his hat and the Spencer carbine, and walked quickly out of the place. Three steps from the cabin he stopped, seeing a single rider picking his way across the open space by the outlet of the lake, his horse uneasy on the naked granite exposed there. As Parrish watched, two more riders came into sight from below.

25

■ Parrish stepped back quickly, to find the others beside him. Sheltered in the brush by the cabin doorway, they watched the distant riders hold a consultation, glancing around in a speculative fashion. It was clear that, while these men knew what they were looking for up here, they were not certain of its exact location. They dismounted, and one man led the horses away. The other two discussed the situation a moment longer, came to some decision, and began to move up along the shoreline cautiously, keeping some distance apart. Presently they were lost to sight behind the low pines that grew down there.

Judith turned accusingly to Phil Bennett, "I thought you said you were alone!" she whispered. "Is this some trick of Dad's or are you playing Cole's game now?"

The sandy-haired rider shook his head. "I didn't bring them here, Miss Judy."

"Then they must have trailed you!"

"Ah, those boys couldn't track a leaking keg of whisky

across a saloon floor. Nobody followed me across the rocks the way I came; not without a dog they didn't."

"But nobody knows about this place except you and Dad!" Bennett was silent. Judith glanced at him quickly and said in a different tone, "Oh, I see. Martha knows, too."

"Yes, ma'am."

Parrish said, "We're wasting time. Is there any way out of here except the way we came?"

Judith glanced at the barrier of snow-flecked rock towering above them to the west and said, "Even if we could get to the horses, we couldn't take them over that. We might make it on foot—"

Parrish said, "That's no good for me. I couldn't keep ahead of them on foot. My lungs still aren't up to mountain climbing, I'm afraid."

She said breathlessly, "We've got Phil's horse here. You could take that and make a break down the trail while Phil and I tried to distract—"

The older man stirred. "Count me out, Miss Judy." He moved abruptly. Parrish saw the gun come out, but made no effort to forestall it. "And this young feller's staying right here with us, ma'am."

"Phil!"

Parrish said, "He's right. If we could all get out of here together, that would be one thing; but we can't make it without a fight, and I don't think you want to help shoot down men drawing Anchor pay, even if they're Cole Hansen's men. I'm sure Phil doesn't. I can't ask that of either of you. And if you help me to escape them, there's no telling what they'll do to you when they get their hands on you. It would be poor repayment for what you've done for me already, if I let you put yourself in a position like that." He glanced down at the carbine in his hand, to make certain it was not cocked, and tossed it to her lightly. She caught it out of the air. He glanced at Bennett. "All right, Phil?"

The muzzle of the revolver dropped. The older man flushed slightly. "I'm sorry, Mr. Parrish. The Old Man asked me to look out for her; he didn't say anything about

171

you except to swear a bit. Like you say, those boys wouldn't be happy with her if she helped you get away from them now." He was about to say more, but a movement of the girl's caught his eye. "Miss Judy, what the devil—?"

Judith had set the carbine aside; when Parrish looked at her she was pulling at her shirt, wrenching the garment out at the waist and partially open down the front. While the two men stared at her, she bent over swiftly, dirtied her hands, and rubbed them over her face roughly; then she snatched at her hair, shaking her head from side to side vigorously, until the long, light-brown strands whipped free. She straightened up to face them, suddenly a begrimed and woebegone figure. She grinned at them in tomboy fashion, tossing the untidy hair back from her face.

"If they believe Cole's story, this is the way they expect to find me, isn't it?" she whispered. "Well, if you're both going to be silly, let's at least give them what they expect, damn it! If we can throw them off guard, maybe there'll be a chance to get the drop on all three of them later, on the trail. You'll play along that much, won't you, Phil?" She did not wait for the rider's answer, but passed him the carbine and then reached out and took Parrish's revolver from the holster and pushed it into his ribs, urging him out into the open. "All right, you dirty kidnaper, move out there with your hands up! We'll teach you what happens to men who mistreat women in this country, cowboy!"

The sunshine seemed very bright in the open; it gleamed on the areas of bare rock. There was no one in sight anywhere. They paused to let Bennett fetch his horse; the man returned, leading the animal, and they moved on down the slope. Parrish's arms began to ache in their raised position, and each step he took reminded him painfully of his fight with George Menefee. He thought of Caroline; there was nothing in the thought to stir him any longer, not even desire. As DeRosa had said, dying, you made your mistakes and paid for them. Then a man rose from the shelter of a boulder just ahead, and at the same

172

instant another stepped into sight by a low mountain juniper to the left.

"That's far enough," the first man said, covering them with a revolver. He was a short, keg-like individual whose thick, curling black beard obscured almost his entire face, except for the nose and eyes. "What the hell are you doing here, Bennett?"

"Why, I had a hunch," Bennett said, behind Parrish, who stood quite still. The rider's voice was calm. "A thousand-dollar hunch, you might call it. It panned out, as you can see. How'd you find this place, Blackie?"

"Why, Cole got it out of that stuck-up wife of his that the sister used to have a kind of kid's hide-out up this way. He sent us to check up on it, figuring that the dude would be needing to hole up somewhere and might have made her bring him here." The bearded man studied Judith at length, and Parrish understood that the disordered shirt had not escaped his attention. He licked his lips. "You're safe now, Miss Judy," he said, averting his eyes with a belated show of respectful embarrassment. "You can put up the gun now. We'll take care of the ba—the coyote from here."

Judith spoke sharply: "I had to wait long enough for *somebody* to take care of him, and I'm certainly not going to let him out of my sight now until I see him safely in jail!"

Bennett's voice chimed in: "Don't try to be a hog now, Blackie. I caught him and the reward's mine."

Blackie hesitated, and watching the bearded, sly-eyed face, Parrish knew suddenly that this whole thing was going terribly wrong. Then the burly man grinned. "Ah, hell, I wouldn't try to do you out of it, Phil. How could I, when Miss Judy's right here to say who gets the credit?"

Blackie made the slightest nodding gesture with his head; on the heels of the motion, the second man fired. Parrish heard the full-throated, black-powder roar of the shot from the left. The bullet struck solidly into flesh behind him, leaving him waiting to learn who had been hit; then he heard Phil Bennett gasp in mortal pain. He was turning now, reaching for the barrel of the gun Judith still

173

held in his back, hoping to use the weapon as a club if he had not time to reverse it; but Blackie was upon him before he could complete the move. He was no match for that solid figure; the other swept him aside and at the same time brought the barrel of his revolver down across the girl's wrist, causing her to drop her weapon. Blackie swung back to cover Parrish.

"Just hold it right there, Red. Get those hands up again!"

Parrish obeyed. Judith was gripping her bruised wrist tightly; a tear of pain had made a track through the dirt she had streaked on her face. At her feet, Bennett lay face down on top of the unfired rifle. There was a small hole in his shirt just behind and below his armpit, and a spreading stain around it. The girl looked at him, and at the man who had shot him, and at Blackie.

"But why?" she whispered. "Why shoot him?"

No one answered her. She knelt by the fallen man and turned him over gently. The front right side of his shirt was drenched with blood, indicating that the bullet had smashed clear through his chest. His hat had fallen off, revealing the whiteness of his forehead. The rest of his face was a grayish color, against which freckles showed plainly.

Kneeling there, the girl looked up at Blackie, shocked and uncomprehending. "For the reward?" she whispered. "Do you really think I'll ever let you get your hands on—"

Her voice died away. Parrish, watching her, saw her expression change. A terrible understanding came into it and she twisted and reached for her holstered pistol. Blackie stepped forward and swung the barrel of his gun with calculated force and accuracy, and at the same time the second man, who had circled the group, seized Parrish from behind as he lurched forward to prevent the blow. The girl sighed and crumpled to the ground.

Blackie took her gun and said, "Okay, Red, pick her up. Back to the cabin with you. . . . Let him go, Steve."

The man behind Parrish said, "Ah, do it here, Blackie, and let's get out of here."

"I said, let him go."

Parrish felt himself released. He looked at the man who

174

had held him, a gangling, bowlegged rider with nondescript brown hair and a wide vacant face pulled into a perpetual sneer by the scar of a harelip. His clothes were filthy and his equipment was in poor condition.

"Let's get out of here," he said again, looking at the towering peaks above them in an apprehensive way, as if expecting them to come crashing down upon him. "I don't like this place," he said sullenly. 'It's like being right up in nowhere."

Blackie laughed, "Better look around while you're up here, Steve; it's as close to heaven as you're like to get. God's got his eye on you, Steve."

"Ah, don't talk like that!" the harelipped man protested. "Just because a man likes to go to church once in a while. Just because it helps him sleep at night after—"

"I never had no trouble that way," Blackie said, and turned to Parrish. "Pick her up, damn it! Get her up to the shack."

Parrish bent down and gathered the unconscious girl in his arms; she was not a small girl for all her slenderness, and it was all he could do, at this altitude and in his battered condition, to carry her. By the time he reached the cabin he was dizzy and breathless. Passing through the doorway clumsily, he left the bright warmth of the day for a cool and musty dimness that smelled of damp earth and rotting wood.

Blackie's voice seemed to come from a great distance: "Put her on the bunk there."

Parrish laid his burden down and leaned against the bunk, gasping for breath. He saw Judith stir and open her eyes; they were blank and puzzled for a moment; then her hand went to the side of her head and she looked up at him quickly, remembering. He knew, somehow, the exact price she paid in self-control for the brief smile she gave him then.

"Well, it looks like my idea wasn't exactly brilliant, cowboy," she whispered.

"I've seen more successful ones," Parrish admitted, aware of the men behind him. They were talking at the door. "But I don't understand—"

175

"That's why Dad sent Phil to warn me, of course. He just didn't want to put it into words, not wanting to admit that my sister and her husband. . . . Half of Anchor comes to me when Dad dies. It seems that Cole and Martha want it all."

He looked down at her, noting that the disheveled brown hair had at her forehead been bleached by the sun to a blondness several shades lighter than the warm tan of her face. Her eyes were gray, he noted, something of which he had not been quite certain. Looking at her, he knew a sudden, awful sense of loss, of time wasted and opportunity missed. . . . A rough hand pulled him away from the bunk.

Blackie said, "Lie down, girlie. Be good, now. Steve, keep an eye on the dude; he's tricky."

The hairlipped man came forward with a cocked revolver in his hand. The vague and almost childishly apprehensive look he had shown briefly outside was gone now; instead his face held an expression of eager anticipation, and his brown eyes had developed a dull sheen. He seemed to find it difficult to take his attention away from the girl on the bunk.

Blackie spoke sharply. "Goddamn it, Steve, I said watch him! Put him back against the wall there."

"Lemme do it, Blackie."

"What?"

"Lemme do it. It's my turn. You did the one down in—"

"Shut up!"

"Please, Blackie."

"I said, shut up." The bearded man scowled and his voice was the patient voice one might use to a child. "It's not that I give a damn about it, you understand, Stevie; it's that this has got to look right. Cole wants it to look right. You'd mess things up too much; you've got no self-control. I tell you what, when we string up the dude, you can tie the rope and whip the horse. . . . Shut up, now. I'm not going to argue with you; that's the way it's going to be. Hell, you don't want to have to spend two weeks in church before you can sleep again, do you, Stevie?"

Parrish glanced at Judith and looked away from the

still, streaked mask of her face. Grimly hopeless, he watched Blackie pull a familiar revolver from his belt and check the loads.

"A nice new Colt, eh?" Blackie said cheerfully. "Well, the Pecos Kid seemed to like it; leastways nobody heard any complaints out of the little bastard after it was over. That was the best joke of the week, Red; if it wasn't for circumstances here I'd like to shake your hand. . . . Well, it ain't often a man can make himself two thousand bucks with two bullets. A thousand for the girl and a thousand for you, Red; hell, I'll buy myself a little ranch and settle down somewhere. This is no life for a peaceful man."

The room was silent except for the deep, cheerful voice. Blackie raised the revolver and aimed it carefully at the girl's forehead. "You should have been nice to Cole, girlie. Cole ain't a nice fellow not to be nice to, particularly when you've got something he wants, like half a ranch when the old man dies, which ain't likely to be long now, haha. . . . Close your eyes, girlie." The voice was gentle. "This won't hurt much."

There was a sharp, metallic click as the hammer came to cock, and the man called Steve drew an audible breath and wet his lips, his attention irresistibly drawn to the scene. Parrish saw the gun covering him sag a little as the harelipped man waited hungrily for the shot. He kicked hard, and struck Steve's weapon aside at the same instant; and with a twisting continuation of the movement he had started, he threw himself forward against Blackie as the Colt went off.

His weight was enough to smash the heavier man back against the logs of the wall. The gun discharged again and Parrish reached for it. He felt the blast of burning powder on his hand; then he had the weapon by the barrel and the man's arm locked inside his own. A knee slammed into his thigh, a fist drove agony into the small of his back, and he wrenched the long revolver backward against the finger still caught in the trigger guard. Blackie screamed as the finger broke.

Parrish had the advantage then in spite of the other's weight, and he used the broken finger as a cruel lever against Blackie's greater strength; but a girl's voice cried an urgent warning and he knew that he had been too long with his back to the room. He threw himself blindly aside without looking around, and at the same time the man called Steve, straightening up, on his knees, from the kick that had briefly taken him out of action, put three bullets into the space where Parrish's body had been. Blackie took all three in the chest. They hurled him back against the wall a second time, seeming to pin him there for measurable seconds. His bearded lips opened and blood came out with the words of protest he tried to speak, and he fell to the floor.

Steve stared at the dead man. "Christ, Blackie, I didn't mean—" He did not seem to know when Parrish struck the gun from his hand, "Look what you made me do," he whispered. "Look what you made me do to Blackie!"

Parrish glanced aside, breathing hard, to see Judith coming toward him. He put a revolver into her hand. "Hold him here. Shoot if he moves a muscle. I've got to get out and head off that third—"

A shot outside interrupted him. He glanced at the girl and moved quickly to the door, holding his own gun, reclaimed from Blackie. Out on the sunlit, rocky slope he could see the body of Phil Bennett. It seemed to have changed position, and some distance away from it lay a second body, unmoving. Parrish stepped out and moved down the slope warily. Reaching the nearest form, he turned it over and looked into the face of a man he had never seen before, who had been shot through the side of the head. He stepped over to Phil Bennett, who lay on his stomach, the Spencer carbine shoved out in front of him.

"Did I . . . get him?" the sandy-haired rider whispered without moving. His voice was barely audible.

Parrish knelt beside him. "You got him. Let me—"

"Leave me alone. Comfortable . . . Give the Old Man my regards, young fellow. Tell the old bastard . . . proud to work for him. Take care of the girl. Taught her to ride and shoot . . . good stuff in the kid . . ."

When Parrish returned to the cabin, neither Judith nor the harelipped man had moved. Parrish lashed the man's wrists and ankles and put a gag into his mouth when he began to talk in a wild and obscene way. Then he turned to Judith, who was leaning against the wall. Her face was quite pale. It was the first time he had seen her show weakness, and he was concerned.

"Are you all right?"

She nodded, and let him lead her out of the place. "Phil?" she said then.

"He's gone," Parrish said. "Took company with him."

She whispered. "Isn't it ever going to stop until everybody's dead? I—" Her voice failed; she turned to look at him, and suddenly she was in his arms, crying softly. Presently the tears ceased, but she did not free herself. At last she looked up with an odd and startled look in her eyes. "Don't play games with me, cowboy," she whispered. "I don't want your gratitude or your sympathy. I'm not your kid sister, so keep your distance unless you—"

He kissed her then, even though it was hardly the time or the place. Her lips were shy, as if they did not quite know the way of this. For all her unconventional clothes and reckless manner, there was an innocence about her that moved him deeply.

"Judith," he said, "Judith, I hope you won't regret—"

She said, "There's only one thing I ask, and that is that you never tell me what that girl meant when she said what she did." She did not wait for him to speak, but went on swiftly: "I don't want to know. People don't belong to each other in the way she meant it. There's part of me you could never have, even if I wanted to give it to you; and there's a part of you that I'll never have, the part that even now is scheming and thinking— What are you thinking, John?"

He said, "Why, to be frank, I was thinking about Cole Hansen."

She looked at his face. "Yes," she said quietly, "yes, I was afraid of that."

26

■ The trail led out of the timber at last, and around a shoulder of the foothills. Here Judith checked her horse for the first time in several hours. "Logasa," she said, pointing.

Parrish looked at the town far down where the foothills opened and began to merge with the more level country of the Basin itself. He looked back toward the high mountains out of which they had come, now a rugged and picturesque wall to the westward. He looked at the town again, a toy town with artificial smoke rising from the tiny chimneys. It did not seem like a place where people lived, and died.

"How long a ride to get there?" he asked.

"Two hours, maybe." Judith's voice was flat and noncommittal, almost hostile.

Parrish glanced at his watch. Then he hauled at the bridle of the horse he had been leading and studied the sullen face of the harelipped man, who was tied in the saddle, his hands lashed behind him.

"Steve," Parrish said, "I'm going to turn you loose. I have a message for you to carry. To Cole Hansen. Tell him I'll be riding into town at seven o'clock. At seven tonight he'll be able to find me on Front Street, if he wants me. Have you got that, Steve?"

A faint glow of emotion showed in the prisoner's dull eyes. "Cole will kill you."

"Perhaps," Parrish said. "But having the job done for him is more his style. You can tell him that I'll be coming into town by the canyon road. I'll leave my horse by Bushmill's warehouse. I'll come down Front Street on foot. I'm making it easy for him, you see, Steve. He can have a man with a rifle drop me at any point, the way he had Silas Purdue killed. Or he can send two or three men to finish me off, the way he did Martin Coe. Or he can have me arrested and hanged quite legally. If he's afraid to meet me."

"Cole ain't scared of nobody." Steve said.

"No?" Parrish said. "Maybe so, but I haven't heard of him facing up to any man less than forty years older than himself, like my foreman, Jim McCloud. You wait and see, Steve. Your boss hasn't got the nerve to go up against anybody who's got a chance against him. He won't face the man who got the Pecos Kid. He'll have you and the rest of the crew staked out in the brush, or on every rooftop in town, to drop me as I go by. Or he'll have his tame sheriff waiting for me. One thing's certain, he won't meet me himself. He notches his gun the safe way, by shooting down men old enough to be his grandfather."

"Ah, listen—" the harelipped man said indignantly, but something made his anger fail him. "Cole ain't like that," he said uncertainly, after a pause.

"No?" Parrish said. "You take him my message, Steve, and see what he does. See if I'm not right. Cole Hansen only does his own fighting when it's safe. When it looks like there might be trouble, he sends other men to do it for him, like the Pecos Kid, or Sniper Boone, or Blackie. That's three men dead fighting Cole Hansen's battles for him, Steve. Think it over." He leaned over and cut the thongs that bound Steve's wrists. "Why, Cole hasn't even got the guts to shoot a woman. He had to pay Blackie a thousand dollars to do it for him. Do you think he's going to face a *man* who isn't blind or crippled with age?"

He did not wait for a reply, but suddenly lashed the other's horse hard with the knotted reins. The startled animal bolted down the trail, Steve clinging to the saddle horn. Parrish and Judith watched him gradually bring his mount under control, look back, and ride out of sight around a bend in the trail. Presently they followed in silence, at a slower pace.

181

They dismounted, at last, at the bottom of a shallow, wooded canyon into which the trail dipped on its winding way downward. Neither of them spoke. Parrish looked about him and determined the largest tree near by, a pine some six inches in diameter at the base. He walked up to it, turned his back on it, and paced off twenty-five yards, glanced back, frowned, and took ten more paces away. Then he turned, pulled his gun from the holster, and emptied it deliberately at the tree. The shots awoke echoes throughout the foothills. He walked back to the pine and looked at it thoughtfully. Four of the bullets had made a ragged group about the knot at which he had fired; the fifth had missed the tree trunk entirely. He shrugged his shoulders in a fatalistic manner and glanced at Judith, who had come up to stand beside him.

She said, "That's fair shooting, but what makes you think he's going to give you that much time?" Parrish did not speak and after a moment she went on: "He can draw and empty a gun in little more than a second; I've seen him do it. And you're doing him an injustice; he's not afraid of you. Of you, or of anybody else. It's the one thing that can be said for him; there's no fear in him."

Parrish said, "You know that, Judith, and I know it. But do his men know it?"

"What do you mean?"

"I mean," Parrish said, "that he has to fight or they'll think he's afraid. He can't afford that. . . . It's the one chance of accomplishing something before they take those prisoners out of jail and hang them. I can't engineer a jail-break alone—"

"Alone?" she said.

He smiled at this, briefly. "Even the two of us. And after what's happened, the possibility of getting somebody to help us is very slight. Even showing my face in town would be extremely risky. This way, I have only one man to face instead of three dozen; and if Cole Hansen falls in a fair fight, his crew won't feel it necessary to avenge him, unless your father—"

"Dad won't lift a finger for him," Judith said. "Not after I tell him about those men Cole sent up to the cabin."

Parrish said, "Then that's your job, to take your father out of action."

She looked at him for a moment. "You have to do it, don't you?" she murmured. He nodded. She said, "There's something I want you to understand. Once I said something silly, about you being a clever and cautious man. I want you to forget that, John. And if—if my good opinion means something to you, I want you to forget that, too. Do you understand? It is nothing to me how you do this, nothing at all. You've got to believe that, my dear. Women are not honorable in things like this, remember that. Shoot him in the back, feed him wolf-bait, blow him up with dynamite, slit his throat, or run him down with a team and wagon. I don't care." She drew a long breath, facing him. "You must not pass up the slightest chance for safety because you think I would not approve. Nothing you can do will make me ashamed of you." She stepped back quickly. "No," she whispered, "no, don't touch me and don't try to kiss me again. I would rather not have had any more of you if I'm not ever to have all. Perhaps I'm a coward, but that's the way it is. Good luck, John Parrish."

27

Riding into Logasa by the canyon road, shortly before seven, Parrish found it strange that the town could still seem the same to him. In the light that now had an evening quality the scattered, weathered buildings stood out sharply in full three dimensions. The ruts and hollows of the dusty street were picked out by the lengthening shadows. It was the same town into which he had come, a stranger and sick, three years ago; it was the same town into which he had driven and ridden many times to court a girl who had later betrayed him. Nothing had changed. The place looked the same; it even smelled the same.

He rode up to the side of Bushmill's warehouse and dismounted, tying the white-footed mare to a section of broken-down fence. He eased the cinches and patted the animal and spoke to her, and she looked at him suspiciously, unused to such displays of affection from him. He took the long Colt out of its holster, checked it carefully, and replaced it; he took it out again, examined it a second time, then shoved it back firmly, thinking, *My friend, you're going to have to do better than this if you expect to live through the next ten minutes.*

Then his watch read five minutes of seven. It was part of his plan of action to be somewhat early; so he gave the mare a farewell slap and started for the street. The sound of a vehicle pulled by a galloping horse checked him; a buggy came into sight around the corner of the warehouse and drew up sharply, and Dr. Kinsman jumped out and ran toward him.

"You damned young fool—"

Time was moving; he had no patience with this and he cut the older man short. "Is he there?"

"Listen, boy, I know how you feel about McCloud and the rest of your crew, but you must see that this is idiotic. They didn't teach you anything about this kind of fighting in the cavalry!"

Parrish said softly. "They taught me how to shoot, which should be sufficient. Damn it, Dr. Kinsman, is he there?"

"Listen, boy, I didn't spend three years curing you of consumption to have you commit suicide in front of my office windows!" the little gray-haired man cried angrily. "If you had the sense you were born with—"

Parrish said, "Dr. Kinsman, if you had the sense you were born with, you wouldn't be yelling at a man who's going to be needing steady nerves in a minute or two."

The doctor looked at him for a moment, then sighed. "He's there, John. Waiting in Morgan's."

184

"Alone?"

"His crew and the sheriff have been ordered not to interfere. Whatever message you sent him, it did not improve his temper. He intends to kill you, John."

Parrish said, "It is his privilege to try."

There was no more to be said, and he moved past the doctor to the corner of the building. It took a certain amount of will to push him past the shelter of the wall into the hostile emptiness of the street. He walked into the middle of this emptiness and made his left turn, putting the low sun at his back. This was an advantage he was taking deliberately, knowing that Cole Hansen would give it to him because the man would be too proud to object. *And because it doesn't make a damn bit of difference to him*, Parrish thought, *because he knows he can outdraw me in any light or in total darkness.* Yet a man could be too proud of his abilities, and that pride could be turned against him.

Parrish began to walk now, putting one foot in front of the other deliberately, pacing slowly, pushing his shadow, like a weight, ahead of him. The town had changed now; Front Street was empty for the whole of its dusty length, but each cross street and alleyway held a group of eager, if uneasy spectators, risking death from a stray bullet to see this spectacle. This aroused Parrish to anger, and he thought, *I would not risk my life to see a man killed.* He realized that he was walking too fast, wanting to get the business done with, and he checked his pace and told himself, *Slowly now, slowly. Why doesn't the man show himself?*

Then a tall and wide figure came out of Morgan's still some hundred yards ahead on the left. The evening sunlight gleamed briefly on Cole Hansen's yellow hair as he paused to set his hat squarely on his head in a casual manner. He took a long drag from the cigarette he had been smoking, dropped it on the boards of the walk, and crushed it beneath his boot heel. He said something to the men who had come out behind him, received their laughter and laughed with them, and stepped out into the street still smiling.

185

Parrish, moving forward at a steady pace, felt the tightness of his throat increase; he felt the surge of his pulse shake him with each beat of his heart. This was familiar and he could note and ignore it. He watched Hansen reach the center of the wide street and turn to face him, still some seventy yards distant. Parrish stopped. There was a small pause; then Hansen lifted his broad shoulders in a contemptuous shrug and began to move forward, walking easily, his big hands loose at his sides. Parrish watched him approach, feeling nothing now: no fear, no love, no hate. His mind was cold and clear, working the thing out calmly: *Sixty yards, you can't hit him yet, fifty, forty, don't let him get much closer. . . . Now!*

Now, he thought, *now*, and at last his hand obeyed. Even at the distance he saw surprise come into the face of the larger man. Then the butt of the Colt revolver was in Parrish's hand, the weapon was coming out, and Cole Hansen moved. Parrish swung himself sidewise and thrust his gun out on a straight arm, target-fashion, cocking it as it came level. Something ripped past his head, dust sprayed at his feet, but the reports of Hansen's gun seemed to reach him only dimly. If there was one thing that war taught you, it was that there were times when people were going to shoot at you, and might even hit you, and you had to continue to function nevertheless. . . . He aimed the pistol carefully at the figure down the street, small over the sights and now half shrouded by black-powder smoke. The piece roared and recoiled, setting him back on his heels. *One*, he thought, *You pulled that one, my friend. You'll have to do better than that.*

Already he was cocking the gun. He brought it back down to the point of aim; it crashed again, driving back against his hand. *Two*, he thought, *Now you're shooting, boy!* Again he thumbed the hammer back and aimed the long-barreled weapon with careful precision and let it hang there until the delicately increasing pressure of his trigger finger eased it off. *Three. . . . Four, Slow down, my friend, you're shooting too fast. That last one was wild to the right again. . . .*

Suddenly he became aware of silence. He came out of

the closed marksman's world into which he had retreated and saw Cole Hansen ahead of him, still standing there but no longer firing. The big man stood spread-legged, his gun in one hand, a handful of cartridges in the other. As Parrish watched, the cartridges spilled to the ground; then the weapon fell among them. At last Cole Hansen began to fall. It seemed to take him minutes to reach the ground. The dust welled up about him and settled again.

After a moment, Parrish looked down at the smoking weapon in his hand. Habit and training made him reload the fired chambers before moving forward. People were stirring up and down the street, released from their fear of stray bullets, but not yet quite ready to expose themselves fully, not knowing what to expect from this situation now. They watched Parrish walk up to the motionless form by Morgan's, and he was aware of their regard as he stood looking down at Cole Hansen, quite dead with two bullets in his chest. The big man's gun lay beside him. Parrish looked at it for a moment, dully. He felt no particular reaction yet. One man lying dead in a small-town street was nothing to gloat over. He had lived through bigger victories than this one.

He turned to look at Sheriff Magruder, who had stepped out of the group of men on the sidewalk, apparently with some thought of taking action. Parrish walked up to the man and said, "You're through here, Magruder."

The sheriff looked at him uneasily, but pride made him say, "Listen, you can't come into my town and—"

Parrish said, "If you're a sensible man, you'll go back to your jail, release the prisoners you hold, ride out of the Basin, and never come back. That way you'll live. Otherwise your chances of surviving are extremely doubtful." The stout man did not move. Parrish took a step forward. "You fool, there's no one to back you up now! You're on your own. Anchor won't be behind you any longer; Mr. Wilkison isn't going to carry on Cole Hansen's work, I can promise you that. Look around, Magruder. You have no friends. Whatever you're turning over in your mind, can you swing it by yourself?"

The sheriff's small eyes wavered. He threw a quick

glance to either side of him and seemed startled to find himself exposed and alone. He hesitated, then turned abruptly and walked away, men making way for him all the way down the street to the jail.

Parrish looked about him. The faces he saw were neither friendly nor unfriendly, merely respectful and rather curious as to what his next move would be. He looked at the Anchor riders still grouped about Morgan's door.

"You have twenty-four hours to leave the Basin," he said. "I would not waste my time here, if I were you."

They held for a moment under his gaze; but there was no one to pay them for fighting now, and they knew it and broke, shuffling away reluctantly. Parrish swung away toward Hill Street. The crowd split to let him through. It frightened him a little with its silent curiosity.

A voice he did not know said slyly, "Wilkison and one of the daughters are at the New Logasa House, if you want to finish the job with a rope, Mr. Parrish."

He stopped at this and looked for the speaker, but no man identified himself. He said, speaking to them all. "The job is finished. I do not—"

Close by, a man called a warning: "Behind you! Behind you!"

He swung about, bringing his gun up. There was a scuffle and the sound of a shot; he caught a glimpse of the insanely contorted face of the man called Steve going suddenly slack, losing all memory of hate and madness. The harelipped man slipped to the ground, dropping the knife he had raised to throw.

Tex Kruger kicked the weapon away, holstered his gun, and turned to face Parrish. "You walk too trusting, Mr. Parrish. Keep your eyes open until this scum has left the valley."

Parrish said, "Much obliged, Tex. How did you get here?"

"The young lady got in touch with me through my wife and said you might need me."

"The young lady?"

"Miss Wilkison."

"I told her to stay—"

Kruger grinned. "Why, she don't look like a girl who'd pay much heed to what a man told her, Mr. Parrish. She's up on top of the bank right now, with a Winchester and two boxes of shells. Said if you didn't get Hansen she sure God would."

Parrish glanced in the direction indicated, but could see nothing. He took a step that way and checked himself; there was too much to be done here. After a moment, he looked back at the Texan.

He said, "I was sorry to hear you'd lost your place, Tex. Are you planning to build again?"

The blond man shrugged. "Takes money, Captain. Reckon I'll have to go back to working for wages for a spell. They cleaned us out."

"Would you work for me?"

"I'd be proud to."

Parrish looked at the man sharply, a little taken aback by the ready compliment. He said, "Well, you've got a job as foreman, but I expect my instructions to be carried out a little better than they were last time you rode for me. Sixty a month. We'll find a place for your family. I want you to go over to the jail, get the hands out of there if the sheriff hasn't already released them, and take them out of town. Hire as many more as you'll need. We'll use Box Seven as our headquarters, at least temporarily; later I'll see if Mrs. Purdue is satisfied with the terms of her husband's will. If not, we'll have to make other arrangements; but for the time being we'll work the two ranches as one. Right now, I want you and the crew out of town until Hansen's bunch has had time to scatter. There's been enough bloodshed."

"Yes, sir, Captain." The Texan made a mock salute, unimpressed by the crispness of his new employer's tone. Parrish watched the lean figure move away and found himself smiling wryly; but the smile died as he thought of everything that was still to be done. It should not be his responsibility to see that Magruder was replaced by a properly qualified law officer, but somehow he knew it would be. It was that kind of country; if a man objected to the way it was run, and made his objections felt, then he was expected to take a hand in running it himself. He would have to make decisions concerning Anchor; he would have to allay the distrust of the homesteaders to the south, and come to some reasonable agreement with them. He would have to deal with the lawless gentry back in the Hills. He would have to see Mrs. Purdue; and he might even find himself faced with the problem of how to treat Caroline Vail and George Menefee, if the pair had not managed to make good their escape from the Basin, as he strongly hoped they had.

The crowd had started to melt away, seeing that nothing more was going to happen here. Some men were carrying Cole Hansen's body, on a door, into Gosnell's undertaking parlor. Feeling bitter, drained, and profoundly tired, Parrish turned and made his way up Hill Street.

The clerk in the lobby of the New Logasa House told him, as if it were a fact that should be known to everyone, that Anchor did, indeed, have a suite always reserved —on the ground floor because of Mr. Wilkison's condition —and that the Wilkisons were installed there now. Parrish walked down the corridor indicated and knocked on the door with the proper number. A remembered loud voice bellowed for him to come in. He entered, reflecting that recent events might have affected Lew Wilkison's prestige, his bank account, and even his spirits, but that the old man's vocal cords seemed to have survived the ordeal intact.

Wilkison, who had been sitting at the window looking out at the traffic on Hill Street, swung his wheelchair around to face the visitor.

"What the hell happened to you, boy?" he shouted, seeing the condition of Parrish's face, a thing Parrish had almost forgotten. His fight with George Menefee seemed to have occurred in another lifetime.

"Why, I ran into a door, I think," he said.

"Yeh, we have some rough doors in this country, for a fact," the old man shouted.

Parrish said, "Cole Hansen's dead."

"Ha, that news is old already!" Wilkison cried. He

stared at the younger man fiercely. "So now you've come around to bully me, now that I'm defenseless. You're going to dictate to me, aren't you, boy? You think you've got me over a barrel, don't you, son? The old man's licked at last, eh?" Wilkison studied his guest and his pale blue eyes held baleful laugher. "Why, you little pink-haired runt! Do you think I'm that easy to beat? I'm going to fix you, son. I'm going to show you up for what you are, just a smart-aleck dude who don't know the back end of a steer from a hole in the ground. The papers are being drawn up at the bank right now—"

"Papers?"

Lew Wilkison laughed. "Why, I'm giving you Anchor, son! Who am I to be less generous than that old skinflint, Silas Purdue?" His voice hardened. "You busted it, boy. Now, damn you, let's see you fix it. You turned the nesters and the Hills people loose on us; now let's see if you can turn them back. It's your ranch now. It's easy to squawk about a big ranch, sonny, but just try running one for a change. I'm betting the job's too big for you. You'll go sneaking back East with your tail between your legs, like a whipped pup. Maybe the Wilkisons can't lick you, boy, but Anchor will!"

Parrish looked down at the old man thoughtfully. After a little, he smiled faintly. "You're a fraud, Mr. Wilkison," he said. "Where is she?"

Wilkison grinned abruptly. "In there," he said, indicating a closed door. "And if you think you had trouble with Cole Hansen, sonny, you wait till my daughter gets hold of you."

Parrish walked across the room, knocked, and opened the door. She was at the window as her father had been, and she turned slowly to face him as he entered. He saw that she was still dressed like a boy, her clothes stained and dusty from their journeys. It made no difference to the way she looked to him now; it never would. A heavy rifle on the near-by table made an additional disturbing note against the elegant furnishings of the room. She followed the look he gave it.

"I would have shot him," she said. "But you opened fire

too soon; I wasn't ready." After a moment, she said, "I'd rather have had you hate me for interfering than have you dead."

Parrish said, "I want you to know that it was a trick."

"What do you mean?"

"His gun had no trigger. A slipgun, Jim McCloud called it. You hold it with one hand and beat at it with the other. I saw him do it once. Who can shoot a gun accurately in that manner? At thirty-five yards I was in little danger; it was simple target practice."

She smiled at this. "You have such a funny way of bragging, John; the way you always try to make everything you do sound easy, where another man would try to make it sound hard. To hear you talk, there was nothing to walking into a saloon filled with your enemies and shooting down the ringleader of the bunch. There was nothing to beating up a man who outweighed you by thirty pounds; or letting another man empty a gun at you. . . . Ah, do you think it matters to me?" she cried. "I told you to do it any way you could; I'd have shot him in the back to help you! I—"

Her voice failed on an indrawn breath. She took a step forward, and he went to meet her, no longer weary.